PARADISE AT LAST

PARADISE AT LAST

Brian O'Donnell

National Library of Australia Cataloguing-in-Publication

A catalogue record for this book is available from the National Library of Australia

ISBN: 9780648014669 (paperback)
          9780648014676 (ebook)

Cover and Typeset: Pickawoowoo Publishing Group

Printed & channel distribution:
Lightning Source | Ingram (USA/UK/EUROPE/AUS)

Table of Contents

PREFACE

This latest novel is a continuation of the story of the life of Billy Riley and his sister Maude O'Leary. After a traumatic beginning to life as a teenager, Billy is reunited with his once hated sister. After also leaving the family home Maude has a new career and a new love life with Richard.

Billy continues onwards with, mainly successes, in business and his love of Melissa, a member of his staff. On the eve of his eighteenth birthday, his future life appears quite rosy now that he has, with the help of the local police sergeant, and the County court, finally thrown off the sadistic brutality and dominance of his father Joe O'Leary. He tentatively tries to get in touch with his mother's youngest sister who he has had no contact with since before his mother's death. He and his gardening associate, Phillip, are forever trying out new ideas to make extra profits from the market garden, mostly with some success.

Growing flowers out of season is a dream of both men and if it ever happens should make much extra income for both of them. However, they need to learn plenty of new tricks along the way if, after huge expenditure on infrastructure and energy, they are to cover their expenses, and finally make a profit, in spite of torrential rain and floods. Then when the garden is inundated with a massive storm and hail stones as big as tennis balls it looked like the end, can Billy and Phillip, turn this awful mess around?

ACCOLADES

Once again, I need to thank all the wonderful people who have had a hand in this production. Without their undying support and encouragement of my endeavours I would have run out of steam long ago. I would like to extend my most sincere thanks to my son David who comes to my rescue whenever my equipment lets me down and Chantelle, my Granddaughter who along with my loving wife Sandy comes up with ideas as well as proof reading my efforts. Sandy keeps me supplied with copious amounts of tea and coffee which helps my brain to function better.

Always in the background there are the members of the team at Pickawoowoo Publishing Company who tolerate my stupidity and ineptness whilst sorting out my messes.

I need to say my special thanks to the team at SPUDSHED in Baldivis WA. for allowing me to set up shop in their wonderful new premises, and hopefully, sell my two previous books, "Shake Rattle and Roll and You've got to be Kidding, along with the latest edition of "Escape from Hell"

Also I am only now realising the work carried out on my behalf by the team at Ingram Spark printing and publishing company. Print on demand [P.O.D.] is a great way for a budding author to circulate his or her works. Thank you guys I really do need your undying support and world-wide exposition.

Furthermore, I need to say a special THANK YOU to all my readers for taking the plunge and buying my books. I love you all and thanks for your welcome feedback.

Brian O'Donnell

Chapter One

Maude and her assistant were swapping yarns about the weekend activities whilst enjoying a pleasant tea break in the office. They had been working together in the factory office for more than a year now and have always got on well together Their landlady spoils them rotten and the accommodation was more, much more than either of them were used to, which was very important because they shared apartments in the same house. For both of them, life had been quite austere in the past and particularly so for Maude even in the days before her brother had disappeared. After Billy's disappearance, followed by her mother's sudden drowning, her life had deteriorated into pure hell. Her father, Joe, had taken his spite and hatred of the world out on Maude forcing her to disappear as well.

They were clearing up the crockery when the phone in Maude's office shrilled out. When Maude answered it she received a couple of shocks. The call was from an old acquaintance from her early school days. James Rogers, who firstly apologised for interrupting her at work, by telling her that he had some very important confidential information, which he was quite sure would be of benefit to her. He offered to meet her somewhere private and discrete to catch up on an interesting bit of history. They agreed to meet in the large public gardens in the centre of town that evening. There was a large covered seating area where they could sit without being over heard or interrupted.

When Maude arrived she was surprised to see two people waiting for her. She spoke out quite sharply saying, "What's this? What is going on? This meeting was supposed to be private and discrete. Hang on I know who you are. You lived in our village. down the bottom end near the council houses if I'm not mistaken, and you are Sarah Jones"

The young lady smiled replying, "Yes, that's quite correct, but now I'm married to James

Rogers here. We live in a nearby village now where we garage and service our fleet of buses. I attend to most of the bookwork and run our booking office. After greetings and introductions were made, Maude said, "Ok, over to you James, what news have you, which might, or might not, be of interest to me?"

James quickly told the story of the trip to South Wales and the meal stop down South in the midlands somewhere. He told her that they had stopped at a 24 hour roadhouse on the main road from Gloucester to Birmingham for their evening meal. He then broke in with, "Look here Maude, the last time I tried to interfere in your family affairs I almost got myself arrested. Are you really interested in knowing the whereabouts of your Billy or not? I am quite convinced that he was the chef in the café where we stopped, although he flatly denied it, as you would expect. He has changed his name to Riley I believe. If you're not pleased, say so now, so that I can put this matter to rest. I hope your father managed to get a lift back home because the police forced me to leave town without him, and, as I had a full load of paying passengers on board. I was left with no option. The whole incident was extremely embarrassing for me and could have affected my licence to operate a coach line and end up with a criminal record."

Although Maude was a bit upset about Joe's arrest, which he probably deserved, she made it clear to James and Sarah, his wife, that she had agonised over Billy's fate for a few years and was very eager to understand what went on and where he is now and how he was getting on. James was so reluctant to further involve himself with the affair that he stood up and prepared to leave. The best he could offer was to provide the details of the police station where Joe had been arrested along with details of the officers involved. Hopefully, if she telephoned the Sergeant Trevor, at that station he might be able to fill in some gaps, but he warned her that the sergeant was extremely protective of Billy. He would have to be handled very carefully to get him to co-operate with her. He suggested that she quietly tell her story and leave it to him. He was only guessing of course but he thought the Sergeant would firstly talk to Billy after thoroughly checking out her credentials and reasons for the enquiry. Presumably if all that went well he would then recommend, or not, her application for information on Billy's whereabouts. James refused point blank, to tell Maude which town, or in fact which county, the roadhouse was situated in. He provided only a telephone number and wished her good luck. Maude reluctantly let the matter rest for a few days to give the facts time to sink in and digest. She would need a long time in private, with no flapping ears in the background before she could put the call through. Late on that Saturday afternoon, Penny announced that she had a date with a chap from near her old home so she would be out until late

Maude picked up the telephone at home after Penny had left and called the number given to her by James Rogers. After an exchange of credentials, Maude admitted that she was calling concerning the welfare of her lost brother William O'Leary. She said, "I understand that our Billy has changed his name to Riley for some reason. I am hoping you can fill in any details for me because

I am quite desperate for news of Billy. James Rogers, a bus driver friend, told me he was pretty certain that he had seen Billy working in a café somewhere near your police station. Unfortunately, my old man went crazy when he saw the young man, who he believed to be our Billy, in spite of the different name. He wanted to avenge the indignities that he has suffered since Billy left home.

Dad got so crazy afterwards that he was behaving really badly, and although he never struck me, he made my life absolute hell. Unlike dad, I don't in any way blame Billy for anything that happened. It was all due to dad's vicious nature and savage and unfair treatment of Billy, and maybe some contempt poured on him by Mum and me, that he left home. My old man was always a total pig to all of us, even to my poor old Mum. I believe that she may have actually killed herself. Like Billy she had to get away from Dad. He would have followed her wherever she tried to hide from him. The only way she could escape was to disappear completely, although, at her inquest the coroner brought in a verdict of accidental drowning and due to a total lack of evidence to the contrary it has stuck.

Please sergeant, can we start afresh. I love our Billy, although our early life together might spoil that image. He was a great kid. I am only interested in his welfare. I have agonised over his whereabouts and wellbeing ever since he left home. After all, he is still only a kid and he needs a safe secure environment to grow up in. Can you at least tell me how he's coping? How is he getting his food and has he somewhere safe to sleep at night? And is he attending school somewhere? He was doing extremely well at grammar school here and it would be a great waste if he doesn't manage to keep it up.

Sergeant Terence read out the report that Billy had given describing his escape from home and his journey south, away from his father. He said that when interviewed Billy had shown the police his severely damage back and buttocks, which they had photographed. He said they had given Joe a copy of that photograph and they offered to send a copy to her at her post office box number. He told Maude of Billy's arrival in their town and his 'temporary' job and the café. He was also able to assure her of Billy's comfort and welfare. He ended the call there, saying, "I'll relate all that you have said to my old pal William Riley, leave him your telephone number and box office number and leave the rest up to him. Ok I will leave it there, goodbye Miss O'Leary.

As promised, Sergeant Terence made a full report to Billy, of the telephone conversation with Maude O'Leary, shook hands with Billy and left him to cogitate the possible outcomes should he return Maude's call.

Later that day, Billy got together with Melissa for a chat. He brought up the telephone call with her after pointing out that he would soon be eighteen and then he would be in the clear. Their lives were full and overflowing at that moment and he needed to sort out where he was heading first before adding in any extras from the past. He told Melissa that he and Maude had never really got on, even before the village social club scenarios. Quite rightly, as it turned out, Melissa suggested that Maude had had enough time to realise how well off she had been before Billy left, and now regretted her attitude towards him. Apart from tolerating her father's crazy behaviour she would have surely been burdened with heaps more chores, which Billy had normally attended to. She went on to say, "Billy, only you can decide what action to take in this regard, but, personally, I feel that, maybe Maude has suffered enough over this matter and there should be enough love and charity in your heart to ease some of her sorrow. She no longer has any other family members that she can go to for solace, only you, if you are man enough to handle it." At that point they dropped the subject and settled in for more kissing and cuddling and petting together on the sofa.

As time went on, Billy thought quite a lot about Maude's call. Let's be honest, about their previous lives together. Maude had caused him untold pain and suffering throughout their early teenage years and he still bore the scars as a result. Deep cuts inflicted with a belt buckle never disappear completely although they do heal quite well given time. So, therefore, what did he have to gain by anymore of the same? A more important consideration was, how much did he have to lose if he allowed his sister back into his life? The Sergeant had not presented a great deal of background information, like who was she now? What sort of personality had she dragged from the morass of their previous lives? It appeared that she was gainfully employed running the office for some factory or other and she was comfortably housed away from their old man, who had no idea where she was working or where she was living. Why did she need him? Why could he possibly need her? The answer to all that drivel seemed to Billy, to be, that it was only to appease her conscience for her previous behaviour towards him, an act of remorse, maybe apology even. There had never been any love between them that he was aware of, and he was surprised that she even cared now. After all, there had been a heck of a lot of time betwixt and between then, and the present day, due to his anonymity since leaving home, which had obviously held up well until now when he was of a suitable age to cope with it all.

Chapter Two

The ROADSIDE RESTAURANT, the new name, for the new alfresco extension at the roadhouse had gained momentum. Every weekend it was table bookings only with a mixed assortment of cuisines centred around the new barbecue cookers with more input from the old but now fully renovated and modernised kitchen. Melissa had been elevated to senior cook and she, along with Billy, carried the bulk of the cooking and presentation. They also had valuable back up from Malcolm and the rest of the crew. The old part of the dining room, although now updated, was always busy, day and night feeding hungry lorry drivers who seemed to save up their hunger for a taste of Billy's food. Reluctant though they were, Vanessa and Billy applied for, and received a limited licence to serve alcoholic beverages, but only in the restaurant and only with food. The alcohol rules were carefully policed and, of course, they opened up the chance for more, and different classes of employment.

England had never been a great wine drinking place but now it was beginning to happen and Billy realised that they would need some staff with a good deal of knowledge about different vineyards and flavours and types of wine. It was a bit of a minefield for the uninitiated, like himself and Melissa, who had never indulged in the pleasures, or pains of alcohol consumption. Were they not really diligent they could end up with a cellar full of expensive, undrinkable, vinegarish plonk. All this amounted to the fact that they would need at least one staff member with a palette suitable to assess any incoming supplies to get good quality wines. Malcolm had a bit of a taste for the stuff but not enough to sample incoming wine supplies or call himself a connoisseur. This scenario left them little choice, as they had to find a suitable expert who would not become an alcoholic. Billy received quite a few applications for the post and they were carefully vetted and sorted. One applicant, Andrew had experience as a head waiter in a hotel Restaurant before it burned down. He had scoured the adverts for many weeks whilst working in a lowly restaurant as a wine waiter. He was keen to progress in his chosen career and he was hoping that the Roadside Restaurant would help him on his way. He was amazed that most of the staff were non drinkers but respected their views. His interview went well so Billy employed him on the spot but with a certain amount of reservation and great trepidation.

Alongside all this activity, Phillip and the outside crew were doing a fantastic job, as were the mushroom girls. They had commandeered one of the old barns at the farm and once renovated it soon became a suitable venue for the drying business. A custom made slicer was installed to make the project viable. Every slice needed to be cut exactly so that they dried evenly in the same amount of time. They could not run the risk of some slices still holding too much moisture whilst others were like cardboard. The drying process was working well and had been upgraded to improve efficiency and time delays. Billy, Malcolm and Mel were finding the dried mushrooms were great as they developed extra skills to re-hydrate them and utilise them in the kitchen to improve the flavours of certain dishes like their stir-fries and even some salad dishes. The packaging had improved allowing dried mushrooms to be sold to other establishments, similar to their own, like classy restaurants and hotels. The mushroom growing scenario had caused some initial problems but, as the saying goes, practice makes perfect. They were now producing plenty of first grade mushrooms, which were often sold whole, and the drying house was allowed the use of any excesses and any misshaped or damaged fungi. All this meant there was little or no waste. Almost everything was useable somewhere in the system.

All this activity meant that Maude and her problems were inevitably delayed but not forgotten. One evening a number of weeks later, Billy with great trepidation, was sitting on the lounge when he picked up the phone to ring Maude. Mel moved close beside him and reaching out held on to his right hand. Billy was actually shivering with emotions and Melissa's touch was very comforting to him. Melissa could feel the emotion travelling down Billy's arm and through her hands and her body. Billy and Maude managed to swap details of their current lives without dwelling on the past. Maude was suggesting visiting Billy at his home but he was reluctant to agree to her invading his home and privacy. Maude invited William to visit her but he said time would not permit that to happen at the moment so it was left open for the present time. After Billy hung up the phone he and Melissa just stayed close together on the settee holding hands then cuddling, kissing and petting as usual. Due to the emotions, they were a bit reluctant to take the kissing any further then gradually Billy began to explore Melissa's body. He needed real solace and Melissa was the only person to give it to him. He allowed his hands to wander about her body, caressing her arms and shoulders and because Mel knew he needed lots of love she let him go. Billy's hands eventually found their way into her clothing searching for her warm soft nubile skin and certain private areas. He was terrified. He was so unsure what was, and what was not, acceptable that he moved his hands and fingers very tentatively, feeling his way around in what he knew was forbidden territory. He did eventually slip his fingers inside her bra and fondle the increasing swell of her breasts. Mel was enjoying the sensation but was determined not to let Billy roam too far. He finally reached her nipples and whilst the feelings were sensational. She called a halt after a little while and carefully removed Billy's hand. They continued to sit comfortably cuddling together until it was time for Melissa to leave and return home in her little Morris minor. Billy didn't want her to drive home on her own but she convinced him that she would be ok and she promised to ring Billy as soon as she got home safely, which she did.

After Mel's birthday party everyone was flat out and busy secretly catering for another birthday due the next weekend. Although it was thought, to be a very modest affair in comparison, someone had to step up and fill the void instead of Billy.

Michael, Peter, and Ernie, joined up with Fred and Alison and of course Melissa with Granny Elizabeth cooking away in the background. They were hoping to deliver a great surprise party for Billy at the weekend. On the Friday evening Melissa insisted that Billy drive her in the Morris minor to a big posh ballroom in Chesterham, leaving the Austin van in town in case it was needed to transfer various foods and supplies around town. In one of the top hotels in Chesterham, apart from a slap-up charity dinner and dance there were to be some fun competitions among the dancers. Billy's name had been secretly entered alongside Melissa's for the ballroom dancing segment. Billy was dressed in his penguin suit and looked really posh as did Melissa in a brand new full-length ball gown. Even if they failed at the dancing they would be the envy of many other competitors and dancers in general because of their presentation.

Four classic dances were to be competed for, namely, The Quickstep, The Modern Waltz, the Foxtrot and the Samba. Billy and Melissa excelled at the Quickstep which was their favourite dance and the Samba [hopefully the Wedding Samba] fitted into their accomplishments. The Modern Waltz was acceptable depending on the choice of music but the Foxtrot was their Achilles heel to a degree. Billy led Melissa onto the dance floor to rousing cheers and they danced beautifully to one of their favourite tunes, The following Waltz, The Celebration Waltz, of course, would also receive high marks and as expected the Foxtrot music wasn't among their top choices but they managed a passable display without making any mistakes. They lacked in some of the finer movements and little details and flairs. So it all depended on the Samba, and what a Samba it was to be. The orchestra struck up with the Wedding Samba much to Billy's and Melissa's delight so they gave it everything that they could muster and maybe a bit more besides. The judges were knocked for a six. The expertise of the whole group really was top notch. Every dance was excellent with Billy and Melissa in front, after the Quickstep. Then almost pipped at the post after the Waltz but still had a slight lead. The Foxtrot set them back quite a good bit leaving them in equal third place with three other couples. So everything depended on the Samba. Any of the five or six leading couples could have stepped forward and claimed the prize. The judges pontificated over the final scores and eventually declared Billy and Melissa to be the winners but only one point separated them from second place. In fact only three points separated first from Fourth.

Billy was almost too tired to drive so it was very fortunate that they hadn't far to go. Melissa was asleep before they left the car park. Billy escorted Mel to her doorstep, gave her a massive kiss to say goodnight. She wished him a happy birthday since it was well past midnight again. This was becoming a habit, but a very nice one, so he delayed his departure as long as he possibly could.

Billy had the weekend off so he stayed in bed until late. He thought it was just as well they hadn't planned a big party again this weekend because he was still knackered. A good, long, hot, shower refreshed his brain a little bit but he was still very weary. He was expecting to receive his chef's papers any day now so he had been down the other end of the street stirring up Muriel and Hazel. He wanted a new chef's uniform, a full kit-out, and a new bow tie ready to receive his certificate if and when it became available. Finally awake and showered Billy drove down to the back door of Muriel's place to enquire about his new outfit. Muriel was busy in the front of the shop but Hazel was in the rear emporium as Billy always referred to it. After the usual greeting and banter she retorted. "Don't tell me? You are expecting your new threads to be ready to wear. Do I look that much like a singer sewing machine, matey? Hey it's your bloody birthday today ain't it? Congratulations and a very happy birthday, too. Give us a great big kiss and lots of hugs to get us started. Here you are, get your arse into this lot, and hurry up, I 'ave plenty to do without all this today. I've got a special party to get ready for, so there, come on get to it."

"Who was silly enough to invite you to their party, Hazel." He answered.

"Never you bloody mind young man. I've got my friends and admirers. Are you going to change your gear or do I have to do that for you as well." Hazel retorted.

"It's up to you young lady but I'll need to help you 'cause you're too slow."

Billy's new outfit was perfect as he expected it would be and he looked resplendent in it. The new tie finished it off nicely. Hazel had embroidered the word CHEF across the right breast. "Come on then let's just show Muriel then you can get it off and packed back into its box until you need it."

"Like hell I will, this lot stays on so I can show the town your inept needle work, young Lady. Go and get Muriel so I can get going."

"Oh there you are Muriel. Look what silly old Hazel has done to me. She thinks I am going to wear these rags to work in my restaurant." Billy stated.

"Hey Billy you look a million quid in that outfit. All you need to do now is try and get that sustificate thingy to go with it. How about you give us both a great big hug apiece then bugger off out of our way. We have work to do here if we're ever going to get to this shindig tonight. Oh and by the way; happy birthday and many happy returns"

"Oh God Muriel don't tell me you've been

invited to the same shindig as Hazel. There must be some pretty desperate people around this town these days."

Billy decided to exit very smartly in case these girls knocked him about and got blood all over his posh outfit. He went home for a coffee and a bun or two then it was nearly time to drive to the café and check the night's work. He was about to change out of his finery when he thought, what the hell? This will do for tonight. I just have to walk in and wave the flag about a bit to keep the staff on their toes. I shouldn't get it messed up if I'm careful. Just then Mel walked in shouting, "Come on William, time to go. Shit, look at you, you're not even dressed yet. Don't you want to go out tonight?"

"Go! Go where to? I've got the night off, remember. We'll just stay in here, for lots of kisses and cuddles. That would be a damn sight better than going out somewhere."

"What the hell? You're taking me out to a big shindig in town tonight whether you like it or not, mate. If you think I am going to sit around here watching the television all night you have another think coming" Retorted Melissa

Billy looked at himself in the mirror then decided, "To heck with them all, this outfit was brand new and spotlessly clean even though it was a bit bizarre. He spun round saying. "I hope you're dragging me out to a fancy dress do where I can wear my new Chef's uniform. Doesn't it look smashing my love, not to just some silly old party."

Mel spat back at him and shouted, "Come on Billy we're late enough already. We'll miss the best bits if you don't get a move on. Come on get into my car, now, please. We'll take the Morris not your crummy old Austin. Don't worry about your outfit you do look smashing in it anyway."

Mel drove them around to the rear door of the restaurant because that was the venue for the shindig that everybody was raving about and Billy was the guest of honour. Most of the town were there including Michael, Peter, and Ernie, also would you believe it Muriel and Hazel. He thought about rushing back to the farm to change then thought "What the heck? Who cares anyway?" A great feast had been cooked up and set out just as last weekend. Once they were all stuffed full of grub, Vanessa mounted the stage. She told the story of Billy's sudden advent into her life and business in the middle of a massive rain storm. On a very dark night. He was like a ghost or some sort of demon appearing from some dismal old cellar, or someplace else. and he proceeded to take over her business and her life. She congratulated Billy and wished him a happy birthday, wrapped her arms around him and gave him one of her special hugs and kissed him soundly on his lips. She could have continued with that all night but then she stopped short as she spotted Melissa's warning glare and invited the Principal of the local college to join her on the stage. After a short pre-amble he called Billy over to join him. He congratulated him on his course of study to become a chef and presented him with his final certification and a special tall chef's hat, then shook his hand vigorously. Billy was stunned; what a surprise, and tonight of all nights. It turned out that a panel of three examiners had been invited to attend an impromptu, dinner celebration at the restaurant, without any of the staff realising what was afoot. They were so impressed that they decided to award him the honour of calling himself 'Chef Billy Riley'.

After a huge drum roll Vanessa asked Billy to open all the presents on the table and there was huge heap of them. He first opened the smallest of the packages noticing that it was from Melissa. She had bought him the very special wristwatch that he had admired in the jeweller's shop when he enquired about his presents for her. He thanked her profusely, mainly with kisses. Once Billy had carefully opened and admired all the presents the band leader signalled to the drummer and he began another drum roll as the wait staff wheeled out the borrowed silver trolley again complete with another three-tier cake on board. It was equally as great as the one Billy had made for Melissa; may be even better. He realised that there was only one person around about here who could have designed and concocted this magnificent sculpture. He jumped down from the stage picked up Granny Elizabeth and kissed her soundly. It must have taken her all her stamina and fortitude to complete this magnificent creation but it was fantastic. Everyone was just beginning to settle down again when Vanessa recalled Billy back to the stage. Holding both of his hands in her hands and looking straight into his eyes she thanked Billy from the bottom of her heart for all his hard work, all his ideas, and all his leadership that had taken the roadhouse from success to success. She said formally, "William Riley nee my old mate 'Billy the kid', I thank you from the bottom of my heart. I could never have even begun to resurrect the mess that you witnessed on your first night here and quite a few after that. Most of what we see here tonight is due to you and all those hours and hours that you toiled away to pull it all together. Congratulations Billy and to say a special thankyou I have had my solicitors draw up this official agreement. William Riley, you are now the proud owner of half of this roadhouse. We are equal partners from now on pal."

There was a spontaneous outburst of applause, cheering and clapping wishing Billy happy birthday and congratulations concerning the affairs of the roadhouse. Melissa jumped back on stage took Billy's hands from Vanessa saying, "Ok Vanessa let him go. He is mine, all mine, except when he is working with you then you can borrow half of him." Poor Billy he was totally stunned. This was all too much to take onboard at once. It would take a few weeks before all tonight's accolades soaked in through his thick skin. He could not think who to thank first. He decided to thank them all together. He took the microphone from Vanessa, and after a short pause to gain his breath and composure said, I would like to thank you all personally and I will do over time but just for now I'd like to say thank you with all my heart. Thank you all for loving me and being here tonight; even if you did only come for a free feed. I love each and every one of you. I can't understand how this all has happened. I have moved on from a life of pure hell to a life full of love and devotion. Love cannot be bought. It has to be earned and given freely and without reservation and that is what I receive every day here in this magnificent town. I came here a pauper and a total stranger and now I own the whole town, thankyou everyone for your love and devotion. The guests roared out at the top of their voices, congratulating him cheering him on and followed of course with that famous song about, "He's Jolly Good Fellow", and all that.

Everyone thought that was probably the end of the official ceremonies but there was a little more to come yet. Sergeant Terence pushed his way forward through the crowd and took the young lady, who's hand he was holding, up onto the stage to meet Billy, before saying, "You two know one another. You need no introduction from me. You need to look out for each other from now on, because you have no-one else to do it for you." He shook Billy by the hand and said. "Well done mate, congratulations for everything and happy Eighteenth birthday."

Maude said, "Well done from me too Billy, I've no need to ask you how your life has settled down in the aftermath of your life in Yorkshire. After all that adulation, it's so obvious for everyone to see." She turned to look at Melissa and said, "I take it this lovely young lady is your girlfriend?"

"This is Melissa, Maude. She used to be my pupil, and she was my employee, then she became my girlfriend as you observed, but since last weekend she has become my fiancé and promised to marry me. We intend to get married as soon as we can arrange all the details and find somewhere to live." Billy folded Maude into his arms and hugged her comfortably to his breast. He realised that if he did not somehow stop all these tears they would have another flood on their hands. Many of the guests were weeping unashamedly. Lots of their friends and Melissa's family crowded onto the stage to get a piece of the action. Eventually Billy and Melissa escaped from the stage and Vanessa asked Billy to cut the cake so they could all enjoy a slice or two. Billy with Melissa's help called Granny Elizabeth over to the cake stand where Billy delivered a smashing great kiss to her before stating, "This is for you Granny Elizabeth, we love you dearly, thankyou Gran you're a real treasure." With that they sliced the cake in the traditional way with all three holding the knife. Someone signalled the orchestra so the dancing could begin. Billy asked Melissa for the first waltz, The Anniversary Waltz, of course. Once the dance was over they caught up with Maude and Penny, her workmate. Billy said, "You've had a heck of a day already but there's still a lot more to come. Have you organised somewhere to camp for the night? I assume you have to get back tomorrow night ready for work on Monday morning."

Maude replied, "Unfortunately, that's quite true. There would be a heck of a panic with both of us out of the office. But no, we haven't booked in anywhere yet. The motel was already full up. We'll have to try both of the hotels next. Do you have a telephone that I can use please?"

"Oh, I'm sure we can do better than that. Can you see Vanessa around anywhere? There she is over there dancing with our Sergeant of police, I'll call her over." When Vanessa was free she joined them for a chat.

William asked her, "Do we have the spare rooms made up by any chance? Maude and Penny need somewhere to camp for the night because the motel is full up, some conference or something."

"Of course, we do. I thought we might need it tonight so the room next to yours is made up, and I put a couple of hot water bottles in to air it off. There are two more rooms available that only need linen if needed. When they are ready to leave, put them in the one next to you if they're happy to share, if not I'll soon get another one ready."

Maude and Penny spoke together assuring Vanessa that they were quite happy to share a double bed. They thanked her and Billy profusely. The dancing continued at a pace until very late. Both girls were very tired after their long trip so Vanessa ran them out to the farm, showed them the spare room and the other facilities then returned to the party.

Next morning Billy had to wake the girls, Maude never was good at early mornings anyway and Penny was weary after yesterday. He and Vanessa cooked up a fried breakfast with all the trimmings and lots of toast to set the girls up right for the long drive home. It turned out that both girls were capable drivers and would share the load. They said it would take them about 6 hrs or so with only short rests. Maude owned a ford Cortina, which was quite new and in top order. Her previous work mates had organised it and serviced it on the cheap for her. By 10 o'clock they were ready to leave after promising to follow this visit with plenty more. Before they left Billy suggested that in future Maude should travel down on the overnight train and he would collect her from the station so they could have more time together. Presumably Penny could drive her to Harrogate station after work then she could hop on the train to Haversby where Billy or another of their crew would collect her. He was pretty sure a return train ticket would be much cheaper than petrol, and she would arrive fresh and rested instead of tired from driving all that way.

Chapter Three

The following weekend Penny went out dancing with her old school friend and neighbour, Frank Barton, and she reported to Maude that she had enjoyed a fantastic night out at one of the top ballrooms in the district. She was quite excited when she told Maude about Frank's work mate, Richard Robinson. Apparently Richard bumped into them at the ball and hung around most of the evening. It turned out that he was a very accomplished ballroom dancer, great company and almost teetotal. His long-time girlfriend had dumped him on the night, even after he had paid for her ticket, and took off with an old family acquaintance, leaving him without a partner for the evening. Poor guy, he was devastated, as you would imagine He hated playing gooseberry and tried not to intrude on his friends. He was uncomfortable taking up some of their time although Penny happily asked him to dance with her when Frank was a bit unsure of the steps in the next dance. Penny suggested a blind date for Maude because she felt sure that she and Richard would make a suitable couple. He apparently had a good career and a late model car. He was now a manager in the firm where Frank was a supervisor. Penny invited both guys around to their home for a nice social evening allowing Maude to assess Richard's potential as a partner. The evening went off very well and a date was organised for the next weekend. Richard volunteered to collect everyone and drive them to the dance out in the countryside. The dance venue had a great reputation. Darley Dale had a lovely hall, very big for a country hall. The dance floor was second to none and they always hired the best bands in the district. They had very tight security to keep out trouble makers who were becoming pests in many local dancehalls. They had a strict policy concerning alcohol consumption both inside the hall and at the nearby pub during the interval. The evening proved to be the 'best' and they arranged to go again the following Saturday. The four of them hardly touched alcoholic drinks although there was a village pub nearby.

* * *

Billy and Melissa were spending a good deal of their spare time searching around the area for suitable accommodation. Once a wedding date was set they would need somewhere close to the restaurant to live. Billy realised that he had caused this conundrum due to the expansion of the roadhouse. More and more staff were needed and they needed housing close to the roadhouse to minimise travel times. One evening they were sitting cuddled up in the spacious lounge at the farmhouse sipping coffee and nibbling biscuits together, whilst running through their latest housing appraisals. Billy said, "It looks like we'll have to settle for a house further away from the café. The only places the local agents have to offer are just hovels and dumps. We haven't seen anything fit to live in even with major renovations. Most have no hot water, some no running water, no bathroom, no kitchen to speak of, dirty old earth closets out near the back fence. It's hard to imagine that anyone could live like that these days."

Melissa commented, "Yea, mum and dad's place is no palace but it is way better than any we have seen. Every week it seems to get worse as they scoured the district and surrounding areas."

Vanessa had just entered the room and as she was settling herself into an armchair with a mug of Milo, asked, "And what's wrong with this house then. Isn't this good enough for you both? It has gallons of hot water, three bathrooms a humungous kitchen, a large dining room and five existing bedrooms with room for more, massive attic space once we clear out all the junk out and endless cellars where you could grow even more mushrooms."

Billy looked on in amazement from Vanessa to Melissa and back again before making the obvious observation, "And it has a sitting tenant in the way. What would we do with you Vanessa? Move you out into one of your barns?"

"Are you telling me that you wouldn't be

prepared to live with me in my house young man, cause if you are you can bug off now."

"I didn't exactly say that Boss, you are still 'Boss Lady' aren't you?" Asked Billy, "Was that an order or just a snide suggestion?"

"Well I believe we three could happily live together in harmony, however I have another crazy idea. You've taught me so well Billy and it seems to be infectious. This house is immense, far too big for me, almost too big for the three of us in fact. So until you get half a dozen ankle-biters there'll be enough room for all of us. I'll need to get Robert, the local builder around with his architect mate, Raphael to see what they can come up with. There are heaps of extra rooms on both floors and sufficient utilities to suffice our needs so how about we create a comfortable two bedroom apartment for me to occupy at the far end, and you greedy pair can share the rest. How would that suffice? I believe it will only take a moderate amount of money to change it around and far less than even a deposit on one of the decrepit old hovels around here. So what do you reckon?" Billy and Melissa were stunned at this generous offer but it made so much sense. This called for huge, three-way, hugs, cuddles and kisses. Billy and Melissa soon realised that the cost to renovate this lovely old farmhouse would be only a fraction of the deposit let alone the mortgage on any other residence that they might be lucky to find and it was full of furniture, fittings, and utensils.

Quite early the following day Billy drove Melissa in the Austin van out to collect her Granny for a quick trip to see Fred and Alison. Melissa was almost exploding with excitement but she kept it under control until they were all sitting around the dining table drinking tea and toast loaded with homemade jam. Billy said, "Go on then Mel, tell them our news. Melissa burst out saying, "We are going to get married about one month or two from today. What do you think about that?"

Fred butted in and asked, "I hope you're not expecting to move in here with us, love. With the crazy shifts you guys work, both of you that is, it wouldn't work out well for us. Much as we love you both, we would not be happy having you coming and going at all hours of the day and night."

"We know that Dad, nobody even suggested it. We are going to move into the farmhouse with Vanessa. That house is enormous and Billy is living there already. He and Vanessa have a great working relationship and Vanessa is happy to work through a suitable financial arrangement with us."

Billy told them of the plan to renovate the old house and split it into two separate apartments The builder and the architect can start on Monday to work out the best way to set it up and work through the costs. Vanessa is even prepared to foot the bill herself but we would insist that we input most if not all of the money. We both have substantial savings and would love to be fully involved. Even if it's not quite finished in time for our wedding, there are plenty of spare rooms, where we can squat until it is. We would probably want to change things around over time but at the moment the house is fully furnished complete with crockery, utensils, linen etc. and ready to be occupied. There are also many other savings on utilities and outside services.

Alison replied with, "Well, what can we say,

congratulations and well done. It seems as though you have worked out a fantastic solution to most of your accommodation problems. All we need to do is get set up for another party, a house warming party."

"Oh Mum, Dad, Gran, isn't this all fantastic? Please be happy for us. I know it's not quite what you had in mind for us but this is much better and it suits our lifestyle so well." Melissa pleaded. Her Dad had one final word as he stood up shook Williams hands and kissed and cuddled Melissa, "Ok, you lucky pair, we love the idea. It takes a worry off all our minds. It's so good to see that you've got everything worked out. We'll all pitch in with whatever needs doing to help you out, such as painting and decorating to save money. Over the next day or two Vanessa, Melissa and Billy had a meeting to discuss costs and finances. The architect had worked out a rough preliminary costing to adapt the old house for their future needs. In recent years a good deal of renovations had already been carried out. The extra bathrooms, toilets, and hot water systems had all been included at the time that central heating had been installed. All that remained was to close off some doorways open others and reorganise access ways. In the hall-way there was a main staircase running up to a cross landing serving all the bedrooms. By simply closing off the corridor both ways with new external type doors, the framework for which was already in place they would create two completely separate residences. The new doors would have to be extra wide to fit the existing frames. The rooms at one end were virtually left without any alterations. There was included a family bathroom, three huge bedrooms one of which originally had a smaller bedroom next door. The wall between the two rooms had been cut through to make a doorway, and the existing doorway into the corridor closed off. By adding a framed wall across the centre of the small room they had created a walk-in wardrobe and an en suite shower room with toilet and basin. All this except for the door across the corridor was already in place. This was to be Billy and Mel's new home. Taking up Fred's offer the whole suite was quickly attended to. The whole place was due for a good lick of paint, new floor coverings and curtains, and whilst the painting was going on, the ladies stripped the old curtains and fixtures off the windows and cranked up their singer sewing machines. Even Hazel got in on the act helping with all the sewing with her machine as well. The girls then had three singer sewing machines between them and they were going at it like crazy. Alison had a fairly new singer, Gran, had an early electric one and hazel had the latest model. As soon as that activity ended Billy arranged for a floor covering expert to fit all new carpets and other floor coverings throughout. Melissa went shopping with Mum and Gran to get new bed linen and great big bath sheets and matching bath robes. All the blankets were sent to be dry-cleaned along with the bed-spreads and all was ready.

They all pitched in and attacked Vanessa's half. She would only have two large bedrooms and the third one became her kitchen dining room. There was an extra room between the dining area and the end wall that was rearranged into a 'Snug' to give Vanessa a sitting room with a television set in one corner. All new curtains were added, new carpets and some lighting fixtures and as Vanessa said she was as snug as a bug in a rug. Later on the master bedroom was remodelled to make room for a small sitting cum T,V. area for her comfort and convenience. The interior décor was magnificent. It turned out that Fred, although mainly painting the outside of houses and offices etc, these days, was in fact a qualified and competent, interior decorator, so most of the colour schemes and décor were left in his capable hands.

There were still a couple of weeks to go before their wedding but Billy had already re-inhabited the best of the guest bedrooms. Actually, it was the very room that he had inhabited since his first night in town. It had the best look out over the market gardens and greenhouses. He was thrilled with Fred's ministrations. The décor really was nice and to his personal choice. The girls had done a great job of the curtains and bed layout, new carpets as well, who needs to get married anyway? Late one evening, Billy and Melissa were cuddled up on the lounge watching something stupid on the television. Melissa was ruminating about this and that then surprising Billy she just blurted out, "I wish this wedding would hurry up. I can't wait to move into this magnificent home with you. It's ok for you, you're already enjoying living here in our new home."

With a big grin across his face Billy commented "What's with all this hurry? We have most of the benefits already. How come you're in an all-fired hurry to get rid of your virginity now, because that's all there is left to sample? You have spent eighteen years protecting it with your life and now you can't wait to get rid of it forever. I thought you realised that you don't have to be married to do that. We can do it anytime you're ready, my love."

"Yes, that typical male strategy isn't it? Sex, sex, sex, that's all you men think about. It won't kill you to wait another two weeks, will it?"

"Hey! Hey! Hey! My lovely girl, it was you who brought the idea up and now you want to hang it around my neck. I reckon it's about time to get you off home before I give you a good spanking. Come on grab your things, I'll run you home to your mother where you're safe from temptation."

"Gosh William, you're just a rotten old spoilsport, aren't you? It's much too early to chuck me out yet." Melissa retorted.

"Ok my love, so you suddenly changed your mind and want to torment me some more. I promised you what would happen if you did not behave so come here, let's see the colour of your knickers then and I'll drag them off you for a bout of fun and frivolity." Said Billy.

"Oh no you don't, I told you that you have to wait, young man, before you can steal my virginity." Retorted Melissa.

Billy remarked, "Who the heck said anything about all that palaver. I promised to tan your backside if you kept on tormenting me and that's what I'm going to do." As Billy made as though to get to his feet, Melissa suddenly jumped up and made a mad, desperate dash for the door. As she swept through into the passageway she turned and blew a big raspberry back at Billy. That was when she realised that she had been duped. Billy was still sitting comfortably on the couch with a big grin across his face again.

"Ok madam, I don't need the Austin until tomorrow and you're on first shift so you take it home and drive it to the shop in the morning. That will save me time and money won't it?

"Oh Billy you're so mean to me, I was only kidding. I will go home now anyway since I'm already on my feet. Are you coming out to see me off or do I need to do that by myself as well?"

"Only if you promise to keep your knickers on. I'll just make sure that I actually get rid of you, so come on my girl, let's do it" So saying he jumped up, moved quickly to the doorway and standing alongside of her he swung around, wrapped his arms around her waist and lifted her off her feet. He continued to shuffle round until he was able to sit on an upright chair nearby and pulling her onto his lap, face down, "Saying Ok young lady, now I've got you in the right position so start apologising and begging for your life."

Melissa was so taken by surprise that she was speechless as William lifted up her skirts to reveal her white lacy knickers, reached up to grab the waist band of them and pull them down enough to reveal her bare white buttocks. He then administered three light taps to each of her meaty cheeks pulled up her knickers again and tidied up her skirts before tipping her off his knee onto the carpet. As you can imagine Melissa was furious, embarrassed and as red as a beetroot. She jumped up slapped him across his face and stormed out without a word. Billy was sure he could see steam and smoke emanating from her body as she went down the passageway. He was laughing so much he could hardly get up off the chair. He followed her to the front door, collecting her coat for her, on the way. As she took out the keys to unlock the door of the van she shouted out at him, "I hate you William Riley. If you think I will ever marry you, you're going to be disappointed." Then she slammed the door and drove off. She was still wearing his ring and the locket though. Melissa was still fuming madly when she arrived home. She slammed through the house stormed up stairs to her room, slammed the door and sprawled on the bed without bothering to undress. She was mortified. She had never been so badly dealt with in her whole life. She recalled the times, only once or twice, that she had upset Granny Elizabeth and had her bottom well and truly smacked but this was different, very different.

The humility of it, the indignity of it, he'll be bragging about it for the rest of his life, our lives in fact.

The next morning her mother called her in time to go the work but she said, "Work could go to hell. She was not going in today nor ever again and that was that. Bloody William could run the stupid café on his own she was going for a long hot soak in the bath." When she finally went down stairs Alison tried to find out what had upset her lovely daughter but Mel refused to speak at all. When she had drank a coffee or two she got into William's van and drove out to see her Granny. Granny Elizabeth had a hard time keeping a straight face as Mel told her sorry tale. She took Mel into a huge embrace and held onto her until the sobs and tears had finally stopped then pushed her away a little and looked into her face. She said, "Oh Melissa you always were a silly, wilful girl and this time it's backfired. William will be needing his van so get away on with you and get all this silliness sorted out. I just wish I'd been there to see your face. There has been no harm done only to your cheeky ego and you've had that coming for a long time. Get out of here and get to work. She gave her another hug and a kiss or two as Melissa left.

It was a very downcast and demure girl who entered the kitchen shortly afterwards. It was after 10 o'clock but that serves him right she thought as she deposited his van keys on the hook near the kitchen door rolled her sleeves and began her chores. She first went out into the scullery and took her mood out on the root vegetables before entering the kitchen again looking for Billy but he had gone shopping without bothering to locate her, and ask her if she was alright. By the time that Billy returned from his shopping trip, the kitchen was running fine again. Having got over the worst of her sulks Melissa had got stuck in to making it so. She hurried outside when Billy returned, to assist with the unloading the van and sorting and stocking everything into the pantry and cool room. When they had finished they both ended up outside besides the van. Billy took Mel into his arms gave her a cuddle and a kiss before asking her if she was Ok. Mel. Burst into a storm of tears and apologised for her sulks. She then looked at her engagement ring and asked him, "Do you want me to keep on wearing this Billy or do I need to take it off now and give it back to you?"

He replied, "Do you want to keep wearing my locket, sweetheart?"

She answered, "Of course I do you said it was mine to keep, remember."

Billy replied, "Yes I did but with conditions. I said you could keep it if you agreed to wear my ring and marry me. Do you still want to do that or is your bum too sore to walk down the aisle with me?"

Mel punched him hard on the arm and stated, "YES! Yes please, the sooner the better or I might need to get another beating. Billy, when I told Gran what you had done to me she laughed in my face"

Billy asked her, "Did you show Gran your bruises, darling, and did she kiss them better for you."

"No I jolly well did not you rotten brute. You're just a great big bully."

"Well I copped a great big bruise from you for my trouble, didn't I. So tonight if you're game, you can come around my home, and I'll have to finish the job properly."

"Enough of this frivolous talk, William. We have lost enough time already today. The new kitchen hands are working well but they still need our supervision."

She then added a comment on the docket books for the breakfast session of the morning, which she had quickly perused whilst he was out shopping. She said, "I had a look over the morning's dockets. They can't be correct, can they? You lot must have added on a heap of extras to make me feel bad. The three of you couldn't possibly have served all that food and drink, it's just not possible. You would have needed roller skates to move that fast. Anyway, the café isn't big enough to seat anywhere near that number of diners as well as the motorists and lorry drivers."

"We can and we did. We used all the tables in the restaurant because the café was so busy with lorry drivers wanting cooked breakfasts."

She replied, "Oh Billy, you can't trick me, the restaurant hasn't been used today, it's still all set up ready for dinner tonight."

"Wrong again, Mel, the two 'M's turned up here for a quick breakfast. They were on their way to their way to work in the greenhouses. They realised the mess we were in and cleared it all away, washed up and reset the tables ready for tonight. We really need to take a good look at the morning trade and consider staff numbers for breakfasts from now on though Everyday has been super busy and Monday mornings are a nightmare. The lorry drivers leave early so they can pull in here for a big breakfast. Also, quite a lot of the local women are finding it easier to bring the kids and themselves here for breakfast on the way to school. We're doing a cheap, low cost brekkie for kids, as you know, mainly cereals and toast, with jam and baked beans if necessary, whilst the Mums have their breakfast in peace. Even our own garden workers are calling in for a cheapie on the way to work some days, and loving it. Mel had the decency to look guilty as she apologised for her behaviour, and negligence. She said, "Oh Billy, I'm so sorry how can I possibly make it up to you."

"Easy for me Mel, I'll just take it out of your hide tonight, when you come around but the kitchen girls and the two 'M's, now that's a different matter. They were magnificent. I'm sending the regular kitchen girls home after the lunchtime rush, and I have organised Ida and Leah, to come in instead. They both need all the experience they can get so 6 hrs, today will help them no end. They will both soon qualify for the fulltime roster and ease the pressure on the others, especially at the weekends. I've asked them to be here by 12 noon to assist with the lunch trade then stay until 6 o'clock.

Chapter Four

Billy was beginning to think this wedding business was mainly women's affairs and nothing to do with him except to find his way to the church and appear all togged up at the appropriate time, on the day appointed. He did however collect and pay for a gold wedding band that his favourite jeweller had on hold. It was one that Melissa picked when he went to buy her birthday present.

One critical detail had completely escaped William's attention though. He supposed, once the idea came to him, that he could manage without the services of a Best Man, although it was traditional. After all he was successfully managing a massive roadhouse and market garden all on his own, so why the hell would he need a best man to fuss around and spoil his day. Most of the current men in his life were already married and not really suitable for the job. Apart from members of his staff he had had little or no experience with single men. Even most of his staff members were relatively new to his acquaintance. There really was only Malcolm, who had been working with him since he and Melissa had started at the roadhouse as trainee students. He and Malcolm were not bosom buddies but they worked well together in the kitchen although they had no social life together due in part to their opposite and unsociable shifts. Billy fronted up to Malcolm and asked, "Are you doing anything exciting next Saturday week in the afternoon, Malcolm."

"I have nothing planned as yet, mate, what did you have in mind? Is there something important that you need a hand with? Oh hell! Isn't that your wedding day? Do you need extra staff for the reception or maybe to hold the fort, here at the restaurant? Is that what all this is about, Billy?

"You might say that, pal, but it's a bit more personal than that," Replied Billy. You see I'm in a bit of a hole. Although, don't get me wrong, your offer to assist with the reception would be well received but the ladies have organised caterers to take over our kitchen for the day to look after our wedding guests so our own casuals can feed the lorry drivers in the café. No mate what I need desperately is someone who knows me well enough to be my best man and keep me out of trouble."

"Hells, bells, Billy, you didn't have to ask. It's as good as done. What do you want me to do? I suppose I'll have to get my best clobber around to Muriel's and get it dry-cleaned. Is there anything else you need? Oh no, I expect you want me to drivel on about something nice to please the bridesmaids telling them how beautiful they are, even if they're not and saying all sorts of nice things about their clobber as well, and dancing about a bit. Hey! I can dance the light fantastic you know Billy, Modern Ball room dancing and all that malarkey really is my forte. You watch me go, I'll show you how it's done alright, said Malcolm whilst going through the motions of a quickstep or something. Who are the Brides Maids? Where are they from? Do I know either of them? Hey you bastard, I bet they are both as ugly as sin. Am I right or what?"

"Can't help you there mate, they're from out of town, Birmingham I believe, cousins of Melissa. Hey, don't call me nasty names yet. They might just happen to be as sweet and gorgeous as our Melissa."

"No chance of me being that lucky mate but we'll have to wait and see, won't we."

"Yeah, there is all that, but you missed out the important bit. You'll have to carry the wedding ring for me and hand it over at the appropriate time. If you lose it you'll have to work here for the whole of next year without any pay."

"Yeah mate got all that and the simple answer is, Yes sir, I feel very proud and honoured to even be asked. When you are ready we can get together and work out the finer points, thanks Billy. I am very pleased to be able to assist you in this, or any other matter, and like you, I adore Melissa so it will give me a lot of pleasure to attend at her wedding to my favourite boss. She is always ready to put her shoulder to the wheel with help and advice. You only beat me to the prize by a few months. I was preparing to ask Melissa to go out with me when you popped the question and stole her from under my nose. Unlike you, I can't afford to get married to anybody at the moment, I haven't even got a car yet so that I can take a girl out, so I'll say, all the very best of luck and good health to you both and thanks again for this honour." The two of them shook hands strongly to cement the deal. Billy was quite sure that the Best Man thing was the last thing on his list. Unfortunately, he had no blood relations around him to run it all past and cross check all the little points. Fred, Alison and Granny Elizabeth had left no stone unturned and they were all set for the big day. Billy placed a call through to Muriel and asked her if she still had hire suits available for men. Muriel had some of her own in store and could get hold of others at short notice, but why would he need one? Billy told her about Malcolm and his suit and said he wanted him to look as great as he himself would, complete with tie and tails, the whole palaver to be exact. Muriel told him to leave it all in her hands and she, with maybe some help from Hazel, would make sure the Malcolm did not disgrace the outfit and spoil the show, which of course was what she did.

Billy saw very little of his bride to be in his last few days of freedom. Her mob were guarding her like a lot of old hens. They had all the excuses under the sun. Something about hair do's, dress fittings, catering, church decorations, hall decorations, taxis to arrange, flowers to order and arrange, you name it, if he had been a drinking man he would have camped in the bar of the nearest watering hole and consoled himself. By Thursday night he was thoroughly pissed off with the whole scenario.

He went home after a very long shift practically exhausted after filling in the gaps in his staff rosters as the ladies pitched in to get this event on the go. He was just enjoying a really good soak in the shower when the doorbell cut loose. Bugger it thought Billy, whoever is it at this time of day. I don't want to see anyone at all, especially not just now. Eventually, after a lot of persistent ringing, knocking and shouting they just let themselves in and stormed upstairs. The doors were never locked in those days. The leading character was his Best Man, Malcolm along with Michael, Peter, Ernie and others hard on his heels. They soon had Billy dressed up and ready for the fray. Fortunately, Billy had stuffed his wallet full of bank notes in case of emergencies and this looked like one of them. They bundled him into the Austin van and headed out to a popular country pub nearby. The pub had one of those newfangled things called a juke box and plenty of room to dance and sing their hearts out. William put his wallet onto the bar for the landlord to extract his money as needed. The landlady had prepared heaps of sandwiches, sausage rolls, hot dogs and all manner of finger food. The men folk did their best to get Billy pie-eyed but that was never going to happen even though some of them tried to spike his fruit juices with spirits. This was because he hardly ever went near any alcohol, and especially as he had a chef's highly trained nose he could smell alcohol a mile away. When the landlord finally kicked them out Billy was still cold sober and ready to drive them back home. He knew they would all be smashed in the morning but that wasn't his problem. He had a café to run and breakfasts to cook so after a minimum amount of sleep, a good hot shower he dressed in his fancy work clothes and attacked another day in his kitchen. It still amazed Billy, each and every time that he considered it, that this, really was his kitchen; or at least half of it was. On Saturday morning, he was out of bed very early and down in his very own kitchen amongst heaps of jokes and ribbing. As soon as everything appeared to be running smoothly he headed back to the farm, into the shower then started to dress as Malcolm arrived with a gorgeous buttonhole bouquet arrangement for each of them, supplied by the local florist. When the time arrived, Malcolm drove Billy round to the church in time and asked him, "Nervous are you pal?"

"No, not bloody likely mate. I'm absolutely bloody terrified. It must be like going to the gallows. There is no escape now I've got this far. Have you still got that ruddy ring in your pocket, then?"

"Yeah you bet, you won't escape with that excuse it's here in my waistcoat pocket. Malcolm patted his pocket then shouted out, "OH! My goodness! I was sure I put it in this pocket. Oh heck, what are we going to do now, mate."

Malcolm turned the pocket inside out but there wasn't even a bit of fluff in it. Then his facial image changed and the hint of a smile appeared as he patted the left hand waistcoat pocket saying, "Ok mate, no need to panic, I must have put the damned thing in the other pocket." So saying, he dipped his fingers down into the pocket and fished out the ring. "You're a rotten sod Malcolm. I'll get you back for that, once this shindig is over just you look out. Just make sure you don't drop it now you've found it again, said Billy."

Malcolm posed the question of Billy, "Is your sister Maude likely to arrive for the wedding? Do you know, mate? Have you heard from her?"

"No but I hope so. Alison was to arrange all the invites so I gave her Maude's PO. Box number so she may possibly turn up. I've told her to travel by train and let us know when she is arriving so we can collect her but I haven't heard anything from her. I hope she hasn't decided to drive down on her own, it's a long way. The last time her workmate came with her to share the driving. Maybe they will both come this time too. We'll just have to wait and see."

At that moment the church bells began to toll and the organist began playing as the bridal party arrived in the doorway. Billy turned to Malcolm saying, "Oh my God the full works, bloody bells, organ, whatever else can there be? At least the choir stalls are still empty. Is there a back door out of here mate, I'm off?

"Oh no you're not, I saw the vicar locking the door with a huge key as we came in. There won't be much pain in here mate, but you will experience plenty of that when the bills come in next week. Let's hope old Fred has plenty of money because most of them should be down to him. At least he only has one girl to worry about, and squander his hard earned money on."

The organist changed tune to 'Here Comes the Bride' and then it was on for young and old. Fortunately, everything went well. The bride wore a Gown of ivory white jewel, and satin with a button lace top, and full-length sleeves. The skirt was floor length with a sash at the waist. The sash was tied with a neat bow at the back. Two of Melissa's cousins from Birmingham were doing the honours as bridesmaids and they looked equally as elegant as the Bride, dressed in ankle length, A line Princess gowns in apricot Chiffon with scoop necks and full-length sleeves. Another of Melissa's cousins from a different family posed as a sweet little flower girl. She wore an ankle length A line Princess gown of fuchsia satin with full-length sleeves and a delightful flowery, lace bodice. Her younger brother was acting, reluctantly I might add, as a pageboy who looked like he would rather be anywhere else other than here. His Mum had dressed him up in a miniature penguin suit with long swallowtails and a black bow tie. He was dressed to kill and looked like he might even do that if he got half a chance. Melissa's dress was a work of art that suited her perfectly and the bridesmaids in matching gowns were a sight to see. Alison and Elizabeth, with a huge input from Muriel and Hazel, had gone the whole hog, nothing spared. I suppose, that, as this was their only chance at this charade, they felt they had to get it right and boy had they done that. They themselves looked a million quid with fresh hair do's, magnificent ankle length gowns and each carrying a fabulous bouquet of roses.

Fred looked so proud and pleased as he walked beside his daughter, in all his finery. No second-hand clobber here, full suit with tails etc black bow tie, the lot in fact. He was fully aware of his duties to his gorgeous daughter and the protocol surrounding this magnificent occasion. Everyone could see how proud he was to be escorting Melissa as she moved slowly down the aisle. Melissa's veil clouded her facial expressions but she looked a million quid, holding onto her Dad's arm with a huge bouquet of deep yellow roses picked from Fred's and Granny Elizabeth's own gardens.

Billy and Malcolm were both stunned. They knew she was a lovely young woman but the vista presented to the two of them was unbelievable as they moved into their places for the ceremony to begin. Malcolm handed over the gold band on cue. Anyone would have thought that he was in the box seat not Billy. He was aware that, although he was the best man, he was only second best in Melissa's eyes. The vicar began with the traditional, "We are gathered here today in the presence of God and this congregation-----. The ceremony went off quite smoothly with all the protocols attended to and Billy was finally allowed to take Melissa in his arms for the traditional, "You may now Kiss the Bride" call. And he did so with much warmth and passion. They signed the register then turned to meet their admiring families and friends as they slowly moved along the aisle towards the doors and the waiting cameras.

There was no shortage of tears in God's house on this day. There wasn't a dry eye in the church, nor outside. Getting quality photographs of the bridal party and the guests was a nightmare. Everyone was dabbing their eyes and wiping tears away. You've no idea what a mess tears and mascara can make to a beautiful face. As the people began to move around outside the church Billy spotted Maude's head among the mob and called to her to come forward. As Maude squeezed her way through the crowd of well-wishers Billy noticed an unfamiliar man moving forward with her. He seemed to be holding her hand. After kissing hugging and sharing greetings with her brother and his lovely bride, Maude turned towards her friend and said, "Billy, I'd like you to meet Richard who has shared the driving with me today. Richard and I have been dating for a while now and he would not hear of me coming alone, either by train or car. We've booked rooms at the motel so we can stay overnight then have a bit of a look around in the morning before we head off back home. We'll see you both at the reception of course. I suppose you can squeeze in an extra guest at the reception for Richard."

"You can bet on that Maude, he can have my place, but he'll have to say lots of nice things and prattle on a bit to fill in time and thank everyone for bothering to come along for the 'Do'."

Billy was stunned at the amount of people crowded round. He said to Mel, "I'm really amazed at the number of people here. I hope your Mum hasn't invited them all to the reception. We can never begin to fit them all in the café. The whole town and surrounding district must be here to make sure you are properly wed. Hey sweetheart, look across the rear of the mob. There's a big group of mainly men out there who look like our lorry driver mates."

"Yes! You're right of course, Billy, I thought I recognised some of their faces. There's quite a crowd of lorry drivers for sure."

At last everybody was installed in cars to be transported to the restaurant, where William and Melissa got another big shock. The wedding cars had great difficulty getting close to the restaurant doorway because the rear parking area was chock-a-block full of lorries from all over the country. The drivers set up a band storm of horns and hooters as the 'Wedding Party' stepped out of the cars. William and Melissa stopped to wave and thank the drivers for coming. He called out to Vanessa saying, "Can we afford to let the lorry drivers have free tea and coffee and maybe free takeaway meals, like curry, stews, soups etc?"

Vanessa had a great big smile across her face, gave Billy a big kiss and said of course we can and we will. They are just as welcome as any of the others and maybe more so than some. They are our bread and butter when all is said and done, without them this joint wouldn't exist. I'll just go and organise it.

William was concerned about the caterers.

He worried that they might not be competent enough to live up to the standard of his restaurant but they came through with flying colours. The roadhouse employees, all their own staff, coped really well with the massive influx of drivers who were very patient and waited their turn to be served. William had been told that the wedding cake was a fantastic show of artistry and dedication. As soon as he saw the cake he knew why everyone was drooling over it. It could only be another of Granny Elizabeth's magnificent creations and what a cake it was. The practice Granny had got from decorating the eighteenth birthday cakes had set her on the road to success with this one. Her poor old hands had worked another miracle. When Billy and Melissa were finally able to get a hold of Granny and put their arms around her, they smothered her with love and kisses. Together the three of them held the knife to slice into the magnificent cake.

Billy was eager to depart for places unknown so the bridal party headed out to the farm as soon as they could decently get away. Alison, Elizabeth and Melissa went along with Vanessa to perform a transformation ready for the road.

Billy's van, [their van now], had been washed and polished ready for the off, but where were they going to? No one, not even the best man had any idea where the couple were going for their well-earned honeymoon. When Malcolm asked Billy where they were headed, Billy looked really serious and commented very loudly so that many of the assembled guests could hear, "How the hell would I know, Malcolm? I'm only the bridegroom. You're the best man. It's your job, not mine, to organise something as critical as that. I've been too busy getting married, in case you didn't notice. You'd better get your arse inside and ring the motel. I'll just drive around town in the Austin until you get a room sorted out for us." Billy quietly gripped Malcolm's wrist and winked to let him know that everything was sorted.

When the ladies returned to the restaurant in their travelling clothes they dumped two large suitcases in the rear of the van. After the traditional waltzes and a farewell ceremony all the guests followed the happy couple out to the van. Alongside the van there was what looked like a brand new red Jaguar sedan. Billy led Melissa round to that side and whispered in her ear, "Did you see all the decorations tied to the back of our van sweetheart. It looks like a mobile rubbish tip. Quite a work of art though. Standing beside the passenger door of the Jaguar with Mum and Granny and Fred shielding her Billy whispered, "Right love as I open the door I want you to feint. Mum and Gran will catch you and slide you onto the seat of this red car then close the door. During all the fuss and hoo-hah Billy popped around to the driver's side jumped in fired up the big engine slipped it in to gear and moved off quickly across the car park and out onto the main road before the guests knew what was happening and could interfere. When he looked back into the mirror some of the guests were shouting, jeering and waving their fists in dismay at having been duped so easily.

Once the Jaguar settled down on the main road heading South-East Mel asked Billy, "What's with this car love? It looks like the latest model Jaguar. It's brand spanking new isn't it? How come we're driving it away and where are we heading to? You left the suitcases in the back of your van where we dumped them. What are we going to wear when we get to wherever we're going?"

"You don't need to worry too much about clothes darling, we are on honeymoon, remember. We won't be wearing any clothes most of the time, and won't have time to change anyway. Don't you worry your lovely head my love, our, 'his and her', luggage is safely in the boot of this car. Mum and Granny packed up some of your favourite gear and we put it in the boot with mine. If we need something else we'll have to go shopping. We my love, are heading for Oxford town, or at least a nice posh motel on the outskirts. This is our car by the way, which by now was purring away happily as it ate up the miles. I bought the jaguar a few weeks ago but could not take delivery of until yesterday. It's not brand new but nearly so. It's not even run in yet. A chap I know bought it for his wife but she hated it and refused to drive it so he had to sell it off quickly and cheaply. I was doing some business with him when he mentioned how pissed off he was with her and the dealer.

Then he offered it to me in passing. He happened to slip into the conversation, I don't suppose you need a nice new car do you, Billy. I went back to the dealer and he said that, once I drove it out onto the road it was second hand. The sales tax had to be deducted and the warranty might be null and void. He would have to restock it and pay another commission to a salesman. He said he would be better off to buy a new one from the factory, however, for a silly price, like about 30% discount, he might just be able to help me out. Rather than let that parasite clean up on it, I tried to think of someone who would benefit from the deal, then you wandered in. "William would you like to buy it. You would need to buy it outright, though. You couldn't put it on hire purchase, which also makes it harder to sell. Do you have that sort of money, William."

We agreed on a silly price and I slipped into my bank quick smart before he had time to change his mind, so here we are heading for Oxford in comfort and luxury, relax and enjoy the ride my love."

"I still don't get it Billy, those cases we

dumped in your van were quite heavy so what was in them?"

"Just some old body parts, you know arms and legs and things that I needed to dump away out of the house before we move in, and they were beginning to rot and stink a bit and the blue bottles were giving them a hard time as well. Malcolm will dump them in the river tonight," Billy said.

"No sorry babe, only jesting, I put the old blankets from the farmhouse restoration in there to weigh them down a bit and make them look authentic before I locked them. I needed them to look and feel real."

Melissa was exhausted and once she got herself settled in the leather seat she dropped off to sleep. The Jaguar was fitted with a radio so Billy turned it on nice and low and so as not to wake Mel, made himself comfortable and settled in for a long drive. The Jag ate up the miles very comfortably and soon they passed through Stow-on-the-Wold and Mel was still curled up in the leather seat sound asleep when they skirted around Burford town then onto another main road near Woodgreen which they passed on their left-hand side. Shortly they branched off to the right following the signs to Oxford. Billy had been to Oxford but not from the North East, nor travelling by car. The train had delivered them into the centre of Oxford from London. His Mum and Dad had brought them down from York with Mallard puffing away in front. They were duly delivered to his Mums younger sister in Cowley for the whole of the summer school holidays because his Aunty and Uncle were about to leave England possibly forever. They were emigrating to Canada or somewhere. The receptionist assured him that he could not miss the motel right alongside the road they were on. Then as they rounded a long right hand bend, there it was, straight ahead. Billy had to gently shake Melissa awake and help her from the car.

The girl at the desk assured them that she had reserved the best room in the house, which was close to the amenities and dining room. She pressed a bell and a teenage boy shuffled in. She pointed to the classy luggage telling him to take that lot and show Mr. and Mrs Riley to their room whilst handing over a key. She arranged for room service to attend to organise meals and any other needs, wished them goodnight as the boy led them away. The room was all they could ever wish for. It was well appointed, scrupulously clean, with quality brand new bedding, and a bottle of champagne in an ice bucket arrived before they had removed their outer clothing.

"Ok sweetheart, who's first? I bags the shower you can have the bath or wait for the shower after me.

"Run me a nice hot bath, darling, I need to get a good soak to remove all this crap the Mum and Granny Elizabeth scaped all over me. Run the bath first up and hope there is enough hot water left for your shower at the same time." So there you have it, he undressed her and she undressed him for the first time. They were both somewhat embarrassed to be naked together in the shower but they soon relaxed as they soaped and lathered one another to remove the makeup and other coatings that Alison and Elizabeth had caked on. They kissed passionately before Mel climbed into the bath then added more hot water and Billy went back into the shower. There was ample hot water left so he joined Mel in the big bath afterwards. Then the two of them showered off again to finish off. It never ceases to amaze people the healing power of a good hot shower or bath. They shared the towels and dried each other off then jumped into the big king size bed completely naked."

Whilst they were still lying in bed waiting for breakfast to arrive, Mel made comment, "The waiting seemed to go on forever but I am so pleased that we did, Billy. That was a fantastic experience, although we were both bone weary. Put that on top of all that happened yesterday and we have a wedding to remember forever. Yesterday was pure magic and it kept getting better all the time. What did you think about the lorry drivers, was that a surprise or did you organise the whole charade? As far as I know, Mum and Dad never invited any of them. They would not have had any of their names and addresses would they."

No sweetheart I caused the lorry drivers to be there but I didn't mean it to end like it did. You see, I, as you know have quite an association with the Headlight Magazine where I run a regular advertisement and sometimes a bit of a story. I told them about your birthday celebration and my own the next week, not forgetting to mention our engagement celebrations as well? Naturally I told them of our upcoming wedding plans and that triggered an avalanche. When we get back we'll have to sort out all the wedding presents because many of them were from the drivers. It'll take us weeks just to write all the thank you cards and post them off."

"I was a bit nonplussed when it was time to leave and hit the road but you seemed to have it covered so well. Swapping cars was a real hoot. The guests were well and truly duped thanks to your jaguar motor car. That is a fantastic motorcar, Billy. I loved riding in it with you driving me."

"That is a great big fib and you know it, my love you slept every inch of the way. I must admit that it was far more comfortable than the Austin. If we had used the van we would both have been wrecks by the time we got here. And about the lorry drivers, the headlight magazine did a short editorial on our day in the last edition. I think Malcolm must have put them up to it. What do you bet we'll be headlines in the Headlight in the next issue. They are always looking out for personal interest articles to make the magazine more interesting and readable" Answered Billy.

"Ok sweetheart, question, why are we here in Oxford, if that's where we actually are? What made you choose Oxford?" Melissa asked Billy.

"Have you ever been here before, love? This is a magic city with more history than the Magna Charta, more fantastic buildings than Rome or Paris. More colleges and universities, more than you can ever encompass, and the river Thames flowing through the middle with boats, yachts and punts galore and more graceful swans gliding by than you are ever likely to see again. Not until you've seen it all, will you realise the greatness of this place, the birth place of education in the British Islands.

Apart from all that I would like to make a special visit to Cowley, which is an adjoining city, the home of Morris Motors. My mother's youngest sister Pamela lives there with my

Uncle Ben, and their brood of kids. I have neither seen nor heard from them since before my mother died so I need to test the waters. No matter what the outcome of that, I will at least know some of the truth. You might end up becoming a widow by the time you are ready to go home. Do you reckon that you will be able to drive the Jag if that happens. I'll have to give you some lessons before we go just in case. Here comes breakfast so we had better get a move on. We can eat in our bathrobes just in case we need to take them off again in a hurry.

Once breakfast and ablutions were completed the happy couple made their way out to the car park. Melissa was a little reluctant to get into the driving seat of the jaguar but Billy insisted. She was used to a manual gear change so that was no problem once the seating arrangement had been adjusted to suit her. Mel was very similar in build and proportions to Billy so the seat and mirrors needed only minor adjustments then they were away. Melissa found the Jaguar extremely easy to drive more so than even her little Morris and a dream in comparison to

Billy's big cumbersome Austin. They drove out around the countryside until Mel was confident that she could cope with the big car. Billy directed Mel to circle around and head back into Oxford. They returned into the motel car park switched off the motor and locked up the car. Billy looked at his watch and said, "Come on sweetheart hurry up or we'll miss the bus. Billy had checked up on the timing and availability of buses passing the motel entrance and one was due about then. Once settled on the bus Mel snuggled up to Billy and asked him, "Ok maestro, what's on your mind now, and why are we riding around in a scruffy, noisy, smelly, old bus when our lovely car is parked nearby."

"Well darling that one's easy to answer. I didn't mind riding alongside you out in the country but I would be terrified in the city."

"So why didn't you drive our car into town instead of me?"

"Aha this must be my lucky day. All the questions are so simple. Once we get into the city centre you'll realise why we are on a bus. You see my love, the streets are ridiculously narrow because they were built for horse-back riding and walking. Unless there's been a big change you'll find that, for the most part, the traffic is pedal powered or pedestrian. All-that aside there is so much scenery to see that a car would just be a nuisance. For most of our sojourn in this lovely city we'll be walking. Every college building is a work of art. Many of the colleges open, at least some, of their premises to the public, especially their gardens, which will be splendid as usual. We can walk besides the river and watch the swans and ducks as well as the boats and yachts. The banks are swathed in weeping willows with branches trailing in the water and birds of many kinds swimming, or darting amongst the branches. Every tour that we make this week will be a study in nature, as well as a study in art and architecture. Come on my love, time to get off and walk. You'll notice all the push bikes parked up in every available corner. Imagine what it would be like if only a small portion of them were cars. As you will see the streets are jam-packed with bikes and pedestrians who seem to wander around in dreamland. Most of the students can't afford to buy a car anyway, let alone run one. It would not be expeditious to attempt to navigate our way around these narrow streets except on foot.

They wandered around the streets and gardens until Mel suddenly realised she was really hungry so they entered one of the delightful little bistros for a quiet lunch before meandering even further around the town. Eventually they had to find their way to an appropriate bus stop to get a ride back to the motel. This was to set the routine for the whole week. After racing one another for the shower they decided it would be a good deal more fun to shower in tandem, which they did. They thought it might save time but that was never going to happen. They arrived early in the dining room to share a fabulous dining experience and they were presented with another bottle of best Bubbly to help digest it. Because neither of them were appreciative of wine of any kind they shared the champagne around the neighbouring tables. Billy asked Mel if she wanted to go out somewhere to finish off a great day but Mel only had thoughts on that big comfortable bed in their room. She said her feet were killing her and she had a whole heap of muscles tonight that she never knew about. She promised to have a really good soak in that massive bath with lots of bath salts thrown in and that is what happened. Having arranged for an early breakfast they hit the sack but not to sleep for some time yet. They had other more exciting occupations to attend to. After all that King Size bed had cost a small fortune for the week so they needed to get value for money, which they surely did.

On the Tuesday evening Mel brought up the subject of their possible trip to Cowley. Billy felt that it might be a bit of an imposition to use up part of their holiday for a personal visit but Mel assured him that it was the most normal thing to do whilst they were in the area. It was a long drive to attempt from home without being sure of their reception. Billy said "Ok then, my love, we'll go for a drive tomorrow morning. Let's hope we find the family at home because of the school break." Mel became a little concerned about the route from the motel to Cowley. Billy said, "It was a long time ago but I am quite sure that this road becomes the High Street without turning off at all. Then if we stay on the high Street it eventually splits into three separate streets and the middle one will take us through into the centre of Cowley. The house is near to the workshops of John Allen Machinery Company. Florence Park is at the other side of their house. Florence Park is a fairly large public park which is laid out in formal gardening and landscaping. Aunty Alice lived at the other side of the park when they lived here in Cowley before they emigrated abroad. My sister and I stayed with Aunty Alice and the house was only a pleasant stroll to the park gates. We practically lived in the park for most of the holidays.

Wednesday morning was bright and sunny and promising a lovely day so after another really special breakfast Billy cranked up the jaguar and away they went. Billy had no trouble finding his aunt's house as expected. He parked in the street helped Mel out and escorted her to the garden door. Uncle Ben had been watering his greenhouse plants and as he returned towards the house for morning tea he met Billy at the garden gate. He was quite surprised that they had visitors this early in the day then realising who it was he reached out his hand and shook it firmly saying "Well, well Billy, this is a real surprise. Come on in your Aunt will be knocked over with a feather. Hello, who is this lovely lady accompanying you Billy? This isn't your sister Maude is it?"

"No not at all Uncle Ben. I'd like to introduce my wife Melissa."

"Your wife? I am so pleased to meet you Melissa, I'm Uncle Ben as you heard. Come on in, the kettle will be boiling ready for my morning cuppa." Welcomed Billy's Uncle. It appeared that there would be no repercussions here after all thought Billy.

Billy helped Mel indoors where they surprised his Aunty Pamela. She stood still for a moment or two before she realised who her visitor was. Then she held out her arms in welcome and she and Billy shared a cuddle. There was a tear or two in their eyes.

"This isn't our Maude, your sister, is it Billy, so she must be your girl friend then."

"No, not anymore Aunty Pam, this is my wife Melissa." Billy told her.

"Your wife did you say Billy? When did you get married? You're still only a lad aren't you. Hello Melissa welcome to our home. Come through into the sitting room and meet our kids. Even you have only met the oldest one, our Billy. You'll remember our Christopher of course but the others weren't born the last time you were here. Come on through and sit yourselves down while I brew a drop of tea for us all. This one is Peter, this is Paul and at last a little girl called, as you would expect, Mary." Once everyone was served with tea Aunty Pamela turned to Billy and said, "Ok you two tell us, when did all this happen?"

"Only last Saturday, Aunty Pam. We are still on our honeymoon." Replied Billy. Our Maude made it to Haversby for the do. She and her latest boy friend Richard drove down stayed the night then drove back on the Sunday. It was a long drive for them but we were all delighted that they made the effort to come."

Just then little Mary yelled out, "Mammy, Daddy, come look. There's a smashing big red car out in front of our house."

After a quick look through the window the

boys ran out through the front door. Christopher shouted out, "Hey look Dad, It's a Jaguar, A red Jaguar. Wow, what a beauty. Wish we could have a ride in it. How come it's parked here in front of our house. Nobody around here has one of these beauties do they?"

Billy said, "As soon as I finished my tea I'll take you all for a ride in it."

"Gosh cousin Billy, is it your Jag? Oh I can't wait. It really is a beauty, are you staying around here for a while?" Once we had all finished our tea Billy took the kids around the estate a few times whilst Mel got to know her Aunty Pamela. They were tickled pink. The kids couldn't stop talking about the car during the rest of their stay. Aunty Pam asked Billy, where they were going to be living now that they were married and what were they going to do about jobs. Billy related some details of his change of life after landing on his feet at the roadhouse and how he had extended it and included the market garden and greenhouses. Uncle Ben was rapt in Billy's description of the green houses and what they were using them for. He was green with envy, so Billy suggested that he and Aunty

Pamela should come over for a weekend or a holiday. He pointed out that they had plenty of room to house the family for as long as they wanted to stay.

Billy explained their situation and his aunty told him that he and Mel were staying for lunch, like it or not, so she could have a good old chin wag and catch up with family news. Billy and Mel agreed so his Uncle took Billy out into the garden to inspect his green house, which was his pride and joy and quite rightly so, it contained a magnificent display of flowers. His Aunt admitted that they had heard nothing from any of Billy's family and they were shocked at the way things had turned out for them. No-one had even bothered to inform them of Ethel's death let alone any other family news. He gave her Maude's address and phone number, telling her that he was sure Maude would love to hear from her. His Aunt Pamela sat alongside Billy and asked him about what had happened to make him leave home. Billy related as much of the family history as he was aware of but there were a good many blanks, some of them deliberate as you would expect.

Maude in their recent brief get togethers had cleared the main points with Billy but she left out huge tracts of time to make it easier to understand. This meant that Billy only knew a very small part of what had happened on the trip to Durham, resulting in Ethel's expulsion from her brother's house.

It was late afternoon when Billy and Melissa said their goodbyes and prepared to depart for the motel after first promising to return as soon as they could get the time off together. They had explained how they were situated with the roadhouse and the market garden. Uncle Ben was quite envious when Billy told him about the three greenhouses. They could have stayed all night but there was a hot shower awaiting them so they reluctantly had to leave. The day had been a great success, considering the family situation before hand, leaving Billy very much relieved and much happier. Back at the motel it was more of the same, pleasant but exhausting sessions in the shower then more in the king size bed. Meal breaks made a great interlude and the meals were very well prepared and presented.

On the Friday afternoon our happy couple found their way into the kitchen where the chef and his crew were busy preparing for dinner. Billy knocked on the door and walked into the kitchen until one of the assistants stopped him and asked him where the hell did he think he was going. Billy and Melissa approached the chef and began to introduce themselves and at first the chef was ready to hurl them out until Billy made a very helpful comment about a particular recipe, which greatly surprised the chef. The chef said, "Alright Mr. Smart arse, what do you reckon you know that I don't. You can't just waltz in here and disturb me and my staff. We have dinner to prepare and don't need any nosy parkers around here."Billy and Melissa both spoke at once saying, "Sorry chef we're guests in the motel and because we are both qualified chefs like you we thought we might be able to learn a trick or two whilst we're here. We're both ready and able to pitch in and give you a hand. Maybe we can pick up a trick or two from you and you might even pick up a few in return."

"You're a cheeky young bugger, I'll give you that, so where do you hale from."

Billy filled in their background and they shook hands before the chef gave Billy one of his knives and set him to work. Melissa watched on for a little while then worked out where she could be the most helpful and joined in the fun. They spent a happy hour or more before heading off back to their suite for a shower and change of clothing ready for dinner. The next morning they went for a final tour of the riverside followed by a delightful meal in the bistro, which was becoming quite familiar to them. They had booked a cruise on the river for their final afternoon. Afternoon tea was supplied on the boat in a lovely bout of sunshine then back to the motel for another fine dinner. They would be leaving for home straight after breakfast the next morning but Billy suggested they return in a more circular route to take in more scenery before they went back home to the grindstone.

He handed the keys of the jaguar to Melissa so that she could drive whilst he navigated. Mel soon began to relax letting the powerful engine do most of the work as she pointed the car in the right direction as described by

Billy. He pointed them in a more northerly direction through Chipping Norton then swung westwards to Moreton in the Marsh and ultimately back home. They had to pass the roadhouse as they approached home, and couldn't resist the temptation to stick their noses into the kitchen. As they entered, the restaurant was set for dinner, and a number of guests were already sitting on the stools at the bar quietly quaffing various beverages. Their staff were really busy but coping well, and the roadside café was very busy with travellers. Billy couldn't help himself as he ventured into the kitchen, which was a buzz of activity. The cook, Jenifer didn't register his presence because she was so busy but eventually she turned around to face him and gave him a surprised look then commented, "Well don't just stand there chef, get your sleeves rolled up and bog in here with the rest of us. Hey how did the honeymoon go? Oh! Please tell us, where did you go to? Did you have a fabulous time and come back to us rested up and ready to rock and roll, or will you both be useless pieces of shit all next week as well?

Billy turned to Melissa who had just walked in behind him saying, "You know what Mel this kitchen has really gone to pot whilst we've been away. It's hard to imagine that we have only been away from here for a week and look what has happened. We're going to have our work cut out to get it back into shape before next weekend. The staff have all died a quiet, natural, death as well, by the looks of it. Still, all that aside, sweetheart, who needs staff now we're back on the job.

"Oh my god fathers, look out. I thought we had eliminated our smart arsed boss but it seems we still have to suffer once more. I expected the honeymoon to be so great that he would never bother to return so we could get this kitchen ticking over properly for a change. It looks as though Melissa has let us down quite badly."

Billy replied, "It's Ok Jennifer, I'm only joking as you are well aware. We are thrilled to bits to return and see everything running smoothly as usual, congratulations on a job well done, we are so proud of you all, carry on with the good work. I'll see you at 6.00am in the morning, goodnight.

The next morning Billy was on kitchen duty but Mel had a lazy day ahead apart from a mass of book work and needed to recuperate ready for the night shift at 6.00pm. Billy had a heap of administration work ahead of him in the next day or so as well as organising staff rosters and running the kitchen. He also needed to sort out where they were going with the greenhouses.

Chapter Five

Mid morning Phillip called in to see him with a few ideas to run before him. He asked Billy about the future of the second hand boiler that had been retrieved from the derelict abattoir along with miles of assorted piping and a heap of control valves. The paperwork that they had retrieved, along with the boiler, Billy had studied carefully with the help of a qualified steam fitter. They found a complete logbook and historical journal, which showed the boiler still had many years useful life left in it and would only need a minimal amount of upgrading to make it work efficiently again. The burners in the fire-box had a dual purpose set up so it could be run on either gas or heavy oil. Gas seemed to be the best option provided the gas company could supply enough gas to fire it up and run it on gas. Phillip and Billy wanted to heat the greenhouses throughout the colder months with a view of producing out-of-season flowers like daffodils and tulips for Xmas. Carnations, and potted begonias all year round, chrysanthemums it seemed could have a much extended life cycle so they should be able to produce blooms for Easter and Mothering Sunday to name but a few, and tomatoes many weeks ahead of normal glasshouse varieties. The critical points that they would need to experiment with to get the timing exact, would take a lot of trial and error and maybe costs. Another point to consider was some sort of daylight, white, lighting to encourage the flowers to bloom on time and the tomatoes to ripen. Both Phillip and Billy were keen to work out all the details so a small, mock up, 'house' was built for their experiments.

Now that the roadhouse was so busy they would be able to sell all they could produce at premium prices. Billy telephoned around to get quotes for energy supplies and mains gas was by far the cheapest if supplies were available in their area. Failing that bottled gas could be supplied but would need a large holding tank on site. Oil worked out far more expensive and also needed to have storage tanks and pumps. The gas company stated the farm would have to be supplied through a copper pipeline which Billy would have to pay for. All this was going to take a long time to come to fruition but much of the expense was tax deductible from their current high incomes both in this current year and future years.

Both Phillip and Billy were quite sure that the out-of-season flower and pot plants would eventually make a good solid profit because they had a built in retail market through the roadhouse. The gas company agreed to supply mains gas just as soon as the necessary pipeline was installed. They were quite sure that their own tradesmen could not start until much later in the year. The gas company workers were fully occupied and booked up well into the future and much as the company wanted the gas contract they could not possibly fit the greenhouse job in and they could not even give a firm date to begin the installation. Billy was devastated at this severe setback because they would not have time to get the project working in time for the next winter. Phillip was quite distressed about the holdup so he seriously considered using Lpg. in spite of the cost of installation and infrastructure. Apart from the flower business, he was looking forward to extending the summer season for tomatoes and cucumbers as well as growing crops like lettuces.

Whilst some production had already been lost, much to Billy's dismay and disappointment, there was still time to capitalise on the situation provided the installation moved along reasonably well with no major hold ups and delays. They received a pleasant surprise when they were seeking the services of a qualified technician to get quotes for the Liquidised petroleum gas installation. A tradesman from Worcester spotted their advertisements asking for someone to quote for installation of the pipe work and valves, as well as supply a large gas tank. Phillip arranged a suitable time to meet the installer and explain what was required. He organised Billy to be available at the nominated time so that they might be able to get the project moving as soon as possible. The gas fitter arrived on time and our duo showed him around the site and explained their needs. The gas fitter, Barry, soon had a puzzled expression on his face, and asked them, "Why are you messing about with Liquid petroleum gas when there's already a gas main coming onto your property for the house. You already have a gas-fired boiler on site in the house. You would have to dig out the existing inlet pipe and replace it with a much larger one. We could then tee off that, and run it into the greenhouse. That would be much quicker and many times more cost effective. Phillip explained the scenario regarding the gas company's fitter and a huge time delay.

"If there is someone around town with a digger we could manage the job in one day. If we're lucky the gas take off point might have a large industrial take off valve, then we can do it all our selves. The gas firm would be able to supply us with a heavy duty meter that they could install on your behalf."

Hey don't look now but there is the beginning of a smile on Phillips face.

"Ok Barry," Billy said, "Give it to us straight. When and how much?"

"I could make a start straight away if you can get hold of a digger and it'll be right to go late tomorrow. I'll have to measure it out to cost the piping but that will be the same whoever does it, also the valves and fittings."

"Ok, we'll organise the digger and get started digging around the existing outlet valve and pipe by hand. Can you get hold of the new metre today or will they have to order one in, and will you be able to get hold of piping and fittings here in town?"

Phillip went for some hand tools and a couple of men to help with the digging. They had plenty of washed sand left around the site on the riverbank and the digger when it arrived could load it on to the farm cart, which had a tipping tray.

"I'll pop around to the gas people and check on the metre but they'll have to install it. We are not allowed to do that. You chaps will need to get hold of a couple of loads of clean, washed, sand straight away to bed the copper pipe into as we go along." Barry said.

Phillip replied. "That's as good as done, mate, we already have a stock pile here on the river bank which we use in the greenhouses and we have a fine screen to run it through."

The outlet from the main pipes had a reducer fitted which when removed meant the new metre would fit straight on. When Barry returned he had sufficient copper pipe and fittings to connect everything up. They had to turn off Billy's house gas main for the day then quickly settled in and got the job moving. Before nightfall Billy's house had been reconnected and much of the new work was complete. Phillip had brought up a couple of trailer loads of washed sand to cushion the new pipes and the gas works inspector called round late in the day to check all the work to date and he was so pleased with the quality of the work that he signed off the whole job and it was ready to go. Billy offered Barry bed and board for the night to save time, and travelling costs in the morning. Early the next morning the team were back on the job and the boiler was fired up by lunch time. That only left the trenches to be back filled with more sand then topsoil and compacted ready to go. The steam fitter and his mate with some assistance from Phillip and his crew were moving along well. There was enough pipe and fittings that came with the boiler to join everything up and plenty of spares left over. Once the steam pipes were all connected the burners were set on low level to give the boiler a chance to settle in for a day or so then the thermostats would need to be adjusted and set to regulate the final temperature. The total cost was much less than predicted and mains gas was far more acceptable than liquid petroleum gas.

Phillip now had the problem of what and when to plant in the hot houses because of the shortened season. In reality it didn't really matter whether or not they were planted at all this season except for the gas costs. This winter was going to be great for Phillip because very little was expected in the way of profitable sales. That meant that he had a free hand to experiment with all sorts of plants that they might not normally grow. He experimented with Begonias, Lilies, even strawberries and lettuce plants. Just imagine the price of very early, out of season strawberries. Even now the first flush of strawberries could, and did bring crazy prices at auction as the top hotels tried to out bid their opposition for the honours to be the first outlet with the new stock.

Billy had been working his brain whilst all this work was going on and he thought he might have come up with another brilliant idea. He asked Phillip if he had ever thought about some free labourers from the colleges. Phillip replied, "Sounds like a great plan but we would never get away with it, would we?"

Billy answered him putting forward his idea. He said, "Don't push this aside without due consideration Phillip. I reckon we could go back to the college principal and offer him a deal similar to the scheme we worked in the kitchen. That plan is still supplying us with skilled and partly skilled staff at the completion of the course and we could do the same with the garden. The market garden is now going to be so diversified that it could give the students a great insight into the business regardless of which avenue of gardening appeals to them personally, and we should be able to get quite a lot of work out of the students as they learn. If any of them aren't prepared to bog in and give a hand we'll shunt them off back to the college. Eventually some, if not all of them should be keen to continue working for us as they continue to increase their knowledge into the future."

Phillip considered Billy's idea and reckoned it just might work. The following week Billy went for a trip to the college for a chat. The principal was ecstatic, pointing out that many of their courses needed a good deal of real, practical, hands on experience and he would put in some time to think it over and get back to Phillip.

One avenue that Billy was keen to experiment with, both in the shelter of the hot houses but also in the fields was tulips and daffodils. This would mean a quick buying trip to suppliers to obtain sufficient seed bulbs because time was marching along. He caught up with Phillip one morning and suggested they each needed to have a couple of days off and go for a long drive to a town called Spalding in southern Lincolnshire where most of the commercial bulbs were produced for sale. Admittedly it was a 100mile journey that the jaguar would easily cover but, just in case they were able to get their hands on a quantity of spring bulbs or some other useful material they would be better served with the Austin van.

Phillip suggested the following Tuesday because Mondays were often turmoil as they recovered from the weekend. Billy checked Mel's roster and she had plenty of leeway around that date so all three of them arose very early in the morning, grabbed a quick feed and lots of coffee then they were off. They got away about 6am so they should be in Spalding by mid morning. Mel and Billy had been trolling through many catalogues and gardening magazines and had quite a list of possible calls. They stopped for a tea break at a roadhouse in Grantham. It was a plain Jane truckers stop and only a poor image of their own. The firm, 'Fontinelli's, also had a similar café near Newark apparently, they were told. The refreshments were reasonable and cheapish but the décor was very tired. It only left them about 30miles to Spalding from Grantham.

They called first into a newsagents shop and managed to procure a local street map, then off they went. Mel had written out the names, and addresses where possible, in the probable order of size and importance judging by their advertising quality and quantity.

The first stop was quite an imposing looking outfit with a presentable sales area. The proprietor was very helpful with information but they were much too late in the season to procure any real quantity of bulbs, but he suggested they try the least impressive of the list because the grower Gregory Matheson had been badly hurt and was confined to a wheel chair for the time being so he might have got a bit bogged down and still have bulbs to sort and grade. This turned out to be good advice and the grower was more than ready to cooperate provided they were willing to get stuck in and help him. He had to rely on outside help because he couldn't manage his fork lift at the moment. Both Billy and Phillip were ready to help out. Melissa had anticipated the chance of getting dirty so put on a coat overall and joined in with the sorting. They ended up with a large quantity of top quality bulbs at a very reasonable price and Billy pointed out the crates of seconds and asked what he would do with them. Gregory said they were mostly viable bulbs and whilst they would each grow and flower he only liked to prepare the larger bulbs for the future so this lot were destined for the compost heap. Even there they presented problems with diseases and parasites. Billy offered to take them all away and get rid of them. He bought the whole lot very cheaply, for next to nothing actually and then they ran them back through the grading machine to improve the quality. By then they had a van quite full of bulbs, overloaded in fact. Gregory was delighted to be rid of the whole consignment. They gave him a hand to clean up the mess and stack the crates and boxes ready for the next crop.

The return trip was somewhat slower because of the extra weight but they were home in comfortable time. On the journey home Phillip enquired of Billy, "Why the heck did you buy all the downgraded bulbs pal. I don't think we'll get time to prepare enough pots and pot up and plant all the others, without the downgrades?"

"Actually I got a bit of an inkling of an idea when I saw all those bulbs that he was prepared to dump. They are all viable bulbs and most of them will produce a nice size flower anyway. I thought we could bag some of them up and sell over the counter then I thought about the middle field. As you would realise it's very sheltered in between the stone walls and I reckon we could end up with a large quantity of saleable blooms that would keep your mob busy picking and packing them for sale. The growers around Spalding don't sell many blooms they pay women and kids to walk through the fields and break the flowers off and drop them on the ground. They only want good big bulbs for sale so they have to get rid of the flowers to get better bulbs."

"Ok Billy, I see your point but we still have to plant all those rotten bulbs anyway. You'd better be ready to bog in and spend days on end bending your back."

"Oh Phillip I thought you knew me better than that by now. You must remember I am a married man now a-days so it won't be a problem, will it. You surely didn't think I got married for love did you."

Mel gave him a great big punch on his arm and said, "You had better rethink that statement, Billy Boy, before we get home or else. I'd knock your block off now if you weren't driving the van"

"Sorry sweetheart, only joking. I thought Phillip knew me better than that by now. I reckon we can quite easily adapt the two row planter. I can fit black polythene dropper tubes to drop the bulbs into the potato trenches and cover them up. They only need to be planted very shallow and if I can find the right size tubing the bulbs just need to be dropped down the tube with the blunt end downwards. I'm sure you have one or two bright sparks amongst your troops who can manage that whilst you drive the tractor."

"Ok, ok, you win but you'd better make sure it'll work that's all I can say. By heck if it works out ok it will make a lot of extra cash for the café and the market garden at a slack time of the year and the staff will be delighted with the extra income. What with the planting and the harvesting, not to mention all the grading and packaging ready for sale."

Billy worked on the two row planter and finally got it working, he thought anyway, but time would tell. He rotary hoed a section in the middle field close to the wall for shelter then, Phillip joined him with one of the staff members, who always seemed to be a bit more savvy than most of the crew. Billy ran the tractor back to the shed so that they could swap the rotary hoe for the planter ready for a trial run. They took out a large selection of tulip bulbs and a good quantity of daffodil bulbs for the trial. It was probably a little early to start serious planting but the exercise might prove viable anyway. The Ferguson tractor did not have the latest levelling and depth control machinery and gadgets installed so everything was a bit of a guess. However Billy finally had a suitable depth set up and away they went. The planter went quite well but it really needed the latest Ferguson hydraulics arrangement to get the best out of it and a much slower ground speed would certainly help.

Phillip raised the question. "Can we afford to buy a new tractor. This old girl is as old as the hills and would make a spare if needed. However, we should not be relying on a machine as old as this to be our main power source to make money, and we are constantly thinking up new ideas that will soon overload the poor old girl. Many a day we need to have two tractors anyway, especially when we're harvesting various crops at the same time. Some days we need to have two separate crews working on different crops at the same time, but in different parts of the garden. Also, let's not forget that there are often times when we have crops ready to harvest, but a need to work the soil or plant other crops on the same days"

"Ok point taken, mate. I agree with you, we often do indeed need two tractors, or even three, available at once so I'll ring around and see what's available and get back to you."

Billy rang around the dealers and checked the papers and farming magazines for advertisements of both new and second hand tractors until he came across an advert for a clearance sale. It was a deceased estate that was being sold up. There was a late model Massey Ferguson tractor of about 50 horse power and many assorted implements to go with it, the tractor was quite new with a diesel engine and had most of the latest design features that they needed. Billy had a chat with Vanessa and she admitted that she had long been expecting to have to upgrade the tractor before the old one let them down. Billy checked with the dealers to find the new retail price and ploughed in the various investment allowances to find a final value. He and Phillip went to the sale on a dismal day. It was pouring with rain most of the morning making things very difficult for the auctioneers and possible buyers. Amongst the probable buyers attending there was a general opinion that the sale should be postponed until a better day but the auctioneers were determined to carry on and as there were no direct relatives of the vendors left to object and all the proceeds would only go into the government coffers anyway because the farm was intestate. By the time that the sale began, Billy and Phillip were soaked to their skins and shivering with cold but the conditions might lead to lower prices so they hung on.

There were lots of odds and sods in the farm buildings to get through before the tractor was put forward. Billy made a sound opening bid for the tractor but well below the lowest figures on his list. The auctioneer was in a hurry, he also was very wet and very cold so he accepted Billy's bid and as no other bids were immediately coming to hand he knocked the tractor down to Billy who was stunned, as were many of the other potential buyers including Phillip. Once the tractor was sold no one seemed interested in the other machinery so it was also knocked down at little more than scrap metal prices. They got the whole outfit for much less than the price Billy had set for the tractor alone. They were not happy with the results on the vendor's behalf but the auctioneer said it would only end up in the government's pocket. Not only was there no will that could be located but there were no obvious relatives to benefit from the sale. The elderly farmer had never ever had a solicitor to act on his behalf so the farm was put into the official hands of receivers to be disposed of. Phillip and Billy packed up much of the small lots into the Austin van and arranged for a transport firm who were in attendance to load and deliver the bigger lots including the tractor and associated machinery. They went home cold and miserable and dived into hot showers at Billy's place, where there was any amount of hot water. Mel had just walked into the kitchen and had boiling hot tea and coffee ready for them by the time they appeared in towelling robes until their clothes dried out. Billy had plenty more clothes but they had no hope of fitting Phil so they had to get his own more or less dry.

The next morning, when at last the rain had stopped Billy went out into the barn to examine the new tractor. It was a Massey Ferguson diesel with a four cylinder engine. The transmission seemed to be extra long for some reason. It had what appeared to be an extension block between the clutch housing and main gearbox making the tractor about 6 inches longer than usual. Billy searched through all the paraphernalia stashed in boxes from the sale where he located the books and manuals of the machinery they had bought including the Massey Ferguson tractor. He quickly realised they had received a bonus prize with the tractor because the extension appeared to be a crawler gearbox to reduce the ground speed for row crop work. He had just fired up the engine when Phillip walked into the barn said, "Good morning Billy, play time already."

"You should mock Phil, have a look at this." So saying he selected first gear and crawler gear then let out the clutch with the engine still idling. The tractor hardly moved forward at all. Even when he revved it up the pace was still very slow.

With a big grin on his face he accosted Phil with the words, "You forgot to warn me the damn thing is fitted with a slow speed crawler gear. How are we going to get any work done at this pace. It'll be great for planting and hoeing the weeds though, and harvesting."

"It must have ordinary gears as well doesn't it?" Enquired Phillip.

"Fortunately for you pal, yes it does. I only have to push this lever forwards to disengage the crawler gears and slip it back into normal gear range. Heck, Phil we had a win alright. It was worth all the cold and soaking and maybe a dose of the flu or pneumonia unless we are lucky."They were both very keen to see it working and soon. They assembled a crew and prepared to start planting. The old tractor was happily rotary hoeing the surface soil to eliminate weeds and produce a nice fine tilth to plant into. A quantity of bulbs was brought out ready and then they quickly got under way. The planter had a fertiliser box at the front to drop the pelletised fertiliser exactly where it was needed close to the bulbs

A week or so later when the tulips and daffodils were showing great promise and growing well everything looked rosy. Billy decided to telephone the bulb supplier, Gregory for a chat. Gregory was very pleased that the seconds had done so well. Billy asked him about his own crop and Gregory was quite dismayed at his results. Due to his accident he had failed miserably to get a good crew together and many of his bulbs were still in the shed. Billy told him about his planter adaptations for planting bulbs. Billy went on to ask Gregory if he had a tractor with crawler gears, he admitted he had a Massey 35 tractor which was fitted with this type of gears which worked well. Billy suggested that they could easily transport the planter on the farm trailer for a quick trip to Spalding if it would help. Gregory said most of the tulips were already sprouting, but he was willing to give it a go. Gregory said he could get a driver to rotary hoe a piece of ground ready for the planter

Billy moved very quickly to load up the planter and organise two of the experienced girls for the overnight trip. Early the next morning they set off for a short visit to Spalding. Gregory and his wife offered the team suitable accommodation for a few nights, as needed, until the bulbs were all in the ground. The planting only took two days then it was back to base again.

Chapter Six

One night the following week catastrophe stuck at the roadhouse. The first indication of trouble was a phone call from the roadhouse night shift boss, Amelia. Billy and Melissa were cuddled up in a nice warm bed when the phone shrilled out. Amelia was in a panic as she reported a massive blaze at the back of the roadhouse. She told them that she had dialled 999 and the fire brigade were on their way. Billy jumped from his bed pulled on some clothes and a pair of working overalls and left in a hurry. When he arrived at the roadhouse he realised that they didn't have too much to worry about. There was a massive blaze alright but it was against the wall at the rear of the car park. There appeared to be a pile of metal objects ablaze. He left the fire brigade to sort out the mess and he went into the kitchen to ask the staff what they knew about what had happened. They were all laughing their heads off at some joke or other and Amelia settled down enough to explain to Billy the possible cause of the fire.

Apparently one of their regular lorry drivers had called in and ordered a plate full of their special little sausages, some bacon and some chips, along with a pint mug of tea and some toast. He had just been served when a group of 'Bikers' entered the café, ordered coffee and a serve of curry each. As they walked past the truck driver the first biker leant over and grabbed one of the sausages bit it in half and swallowed it. As each of the other bikers walked passed they each stole a sausage and or a chip or bacon the last one took the mug of tea in one hand and a slice of toast as well. The lorry driver realising the odds were seriously against him let them get away with it. He had no hope of challenging the bikers as they would surely have knocked his head off and severely beaten him up, so he stood up and walked out and paid for his meal as he passed the counter. He went around into the rear car park fired up his big articulated lorry roared up the motor and began to manoeuvre it around the car park in preparation to leave. Amelia could see most of the action through the window but decided to turn a blind eye. Anyway she needed to concentrate on cooking and running her kitchen. She glanced out a bit later but the car park was empty as the lorry had already moved off after the driver had sorted out himself and his rig then managed to get it pointing in the right direction for home.

The bikers got up to leave soon after the lorry driver, threw some money on the counter and were preparing to walk out when one of them turned to Amelia saying, "Not much of a man, your lorry driver pal, just sitting there, letting us pinch his dinner and not saying a word. We expected a decent bit of a fight for our troubles to brighten up our night. What did you reckon to that then?"

Amelia said in reply. "Yea I expect you're right in what you say, not much of a man, as you say, and I tell you what, he's a shit awful lorry driver too. I spotted him shunting that great big articulated trailer around the car park. There were a bunch of motorbikes parked out near the back wall and he backed his trailer right into them before he got sorted. OH!! NO!! My God!! look, the bikes are on fire." There was a great big whoosh because the spilt petrol had caught alight, as one of the batteries must have shorted out, ignited some of the petrol, and one by one the other fuel tanks exploded. The bike tyres soon began to melt then explode when the pressure from inside burst them open. Whilst everyone was engrossed in the fire the articulated lorry had sped off into the night heading off to, who knows where. Amelia grabbed the phone and called the fire brigade and the police.

Later when the police and firemen had the fire under control the police sergeant went into the café to find out if anyone knew who the driver was and in which direction he had gone. He also asked if anyone had noticed the cab of the lorry and did it have any name or insignia painted on it. Amelia recounted the tale about the sausages but said she was staring out of the window watching the fire after telephoning for the fire brigade. By the time that she looked around the car park it was empty. She hadn't seen what sort of a lorry it was, nor which way the lorry went so she couldn't help.

The bikers came back into the café to give her a hard time, trying to find out who the driver was. Amelia pointed out that they had talked to the driver as they stole his food, so they should know who he was and what he looked like. The police got the message that the bikers had got their true deserts and didn't worry too much about it anymore. They just took a couple of statements and left it at that. Amelia saw the driver a few weeks later when he called in for another meal with his freshly painted rear end and they had a good laugh about it. The truck driver had no knowledge of the fire of course, because he was miles away by then.

One morning about that time Billy noticed that Mel was a bit off colour and suggested a day of rest as she was not on roster anyway. He stopped in the doorway and had a good look back at his lovely bride, then realised what her trouble was, although she herself hadn't worked it out yet. He said to Mel. "Have you been keeping secrets from me lately, my darling? How far gone are you?" How many months have you missed? You realise you've been and got yourself 'Knocked Up' don't you?"

Melissa immediately twigged what he was saying and rubbed her belly, Replied, "Oh heck! I've been so busy I never gave it a thought. I realised that I am a couple of weeks late at the moment but I must have missed the last month as well, maybe even two now I come to think about it. I'd better ring Doctor Madison for an appointment and get a check up. I'll do that today. Come here you brute. This is all your fault. My Mum and my Gran warned me about men like you."

They enjoyed a great big hug and lots of kisses but Billy had things to do and eventually had to leave with instructions to call and tell him what the doctor said.

Doctor Madison thoroughly examined Melissa and arranged for blood tests just to make sure that all was well. He reckoned that she was about 10 weeks pregnant so she had got through that dreaded first semester without any side effects, no morning sickness just a few 'off' days.

Melissa jumped into her little Morris car and sped around to her old home to tell her Mum the good news. Alison was delighted of course and after a nice cuppa and a cake or two they drove out in the Morris to see Granny Elizabeth for lots more hugs and kisses, tea and cakes. Melissa had called Billy at the café and he was ecstatic and so were all the staff members and a few customers. It had taken a little while longer than expected for Melissa to fall pregnant but now it was happening, leaving only the speculation, will it be a boy or a girl. The fact that she had remained in good health to date was a real bonus.

The next issue of course was to set up a nursery. There was an extra dressing room attached to the master bedroom that was not currently in use. The en-suite shower room was alongside the dressing room so all it needed was a lick of paint and maybe some new drapes. Stored away in the attic there was plenty of furniture for Fred to work his magic on, naturally with Melissa's eagle eye watching on.

"Boy, Oh Boy," Billy began when Mel returned, "I'm damned if I can work out this pregnancy lark. This one has hardly begun and already it has turned my busy life into chaos. Yesterday everything was going good, now only one day into this malarkey, my life is a disaster, but you women are in raptures of delight."

Mel put her arms around Billy kissed his cheek and said, "Come here my love and tell me what has gone wrong today."

"It's ok for you women, you are designed for all this malarky, but us men are expected to merge our feelings and sort out our lives just because you got yourself pregnant. Yesterday I was running a busy Kitchen and restaurant with a heap of staff and keeping tabs with the market garden events with Phil. Today my life is in chaos, I hope you realise that I am about to lose my best member of staff from the kitchen. I, little old Billy, left to organise supplies of nappies and God knows what else. Poor old Fred will need to make time for a nursery remodelling and prepare himself for babysitting, as well. Meanwhile I'll have to keep working myself to death to keep up to never ending cries of, 'I wants until the little beggar is old enough to help out in the café or the garden. How old does he have to be before I can start him off working for me? All the while I'll have you women under foot 24 hrs every day, and I'll have to cook my own dinners wash my own clothes. Gosh Melissa what have I done to deserve this?"

Melissa hugged and consoled poor Billy and suggested an extended romp in the sheets to ease his tortured mind. Billy jumped back with a look of horror on his face and pushed Mel away, saying, "Now then Mel, control yourself. Look what happened the last time you seduced me and now you want to do it again"

"You won't have to worry about that for a few months, my love so come on lets relax and blow off a bit of steam while we can." Which, they most certainly did.

The next morning Billy saw Melissa off to work in the restaurant and he headed out to the garden for a catch up time with Phillip. The spring bulbs were all looking good and some almost ready for harvesting. They had to get the timing exactly correct, too soon and the flowers would fail to open and only a day or two late and they would spoil. Phil was strolling down the rows of bulbs trying to work out his next move. He welcomed Billy's arrival hoping to get a second opinion. But first he grabbed Billy's hand and shook it vigorously saying, "Congratulations old son, well done. Will it be a boy or a girl do you reckon?"

"I've told Mel that it had better be a boy so we can put him to work here in the garden. You know Phil I've been thinking about that and I've realised that it probably won't matter. I've seen it here with my own eyes. We employ a good many girls here in the garden, starting from twelve year olds right through to Grandmothers, and they are all good workers and much more prompt and regular than the boys, especially the younger ones. What do you reckon Phil am I right or what?"

"Yes Billy, I can't argue with that philosophy. You are so right. Now what do you reckon about these flowers?"

"I went to the markets yesterday and had a good look around and discussed their stocks with them. There are already reasonable supplies arriving from the Channel Islands with mixed results. Some were obviously picked to soon and quite a lot too late. Also, and very important for us, there was quite a lot of damage due to transport and handling. We should be able to cut out most of that if we are careful. Have you got all your staff organised and has the packaging arrived in good condition."

"Yes we are all ready, so tell me how they should look."

"Ok grab a few boxes and we can select enough for the roadhouse already by the look of them. Do you have a staff member who can bunch them up and pack them for sale. A dozen in a bunch seems to work out well. What say we you round up 3 or 4 people for early in the morning, say about 7.30. Did you get the wrapping paper and elastic ties. We can use the hand cart and pack up the flowers as we go."

"That sounds good to me Billy, so, I'll see you then." Said Phillip.

Next morning the sun was shining down on the world at large so Billy led the crew along the first rows. He explained the flowers going straight into the café could be further advanced than the market ones. They needed quite a lot of bunches for the shop and some were just placed standing up in buckets from where customers could select their own colours and varieties. As soon as they had enough for the café and some to make a start in the market Billy loaded them into the Austin and delivered them. He arranged to meet everyone the next morning to repeat the operation provided the weather was clement.

"When the crew were all in attendance the next morning Billy congratulated them all on their efforts because they had sold out immediately at the market and later at the café. One florist at the market took delivery of the whole consignment and wanted all they could get today. They were in fact, coming to the garden shortly to collect as many as Phil could supply. It was the freshness of the blooms that made all the difference. Getting them straight from the garden meant they would have two or three extra days shelf life. Whilst all this palaver was going on Billy went over to the greenhouses to check the bowls of spring bulbs. Many of the bulbs were in full bud and about to explode into bloom so as soon as the crew had finished picking the field blooms he called them over to begin moving the bowls out to the cafe area which had been set aside for this purpose and organised a load into the Austin van for delivery to the markets. Both venues were ripe to go and the markets in particular were delighted. Some of the local hotels and florists scooped up all of the load between them and wanted more. Phil and Billy were praying for a few more sunny days to recoup their input costs.

On the third morning it was raining quite heavily so they had no option but to ignore the field flowers and concentrate on getting the bowls out of the hothouses. There was another problem to sort out in the hothouses too. The early tomato plants were ready for transplanting and setting up in the ground and supports had to be attached as well. They had to divorce themselves from the field crops, which did not owe them very much since the bulbs were free. and concentrate on the hot houses until the weather settled down again. They had already recouped most if not all the planting and weeding costs in the field crops. By mid morning the sun was out again so hopefully there would be little or no damage to the blooms. Phil organised a crew of pickers and packers ready for later in the day to wade in and pick as many blooms as possible for the market the following day, and any advanced ones earmarked for the café.

Towards the end of the week Billy had a chat with Phil and pointed out that from now on he would have to carry most if not all the work attributed to the garden because Melissa would need to start slowing down and taking life much easier as the baby progressed. However he agreed to try and be on hand should Phil need any support, he just would have to rely on other staff to do most of the actual field work. Phil also reminded Billy that there was much planting and weeding in the garden as summer rolled in. He added that he had a good list of possible hands should they be needed and one of the younger hands was showing himself to be very competent with the tractors and machinery. His Family ran a fairly big mixed farm nearby but his older brothers did not need his services, so he had attached himself to the garden full time and was loving the daily challenges. There was always plenty of tractor work and he had lots of experience in that side of farming. Jeffery also had an analytical mind like Billy and could adjust himself to new ideas, sometimes with Billy's help but quite often on his own initiative. His input took quite a lot of worry and concern off the shoulders of Billy and Phil leaving them free to manage other aspects of their management strategy. Every aspect of the garden enterprise seemed to be running smoothly at that time but as always the weather situation needed to be watched. It could change in an instant and more often than not there was little or actually nothing that they could do to negate its influence on their lives.

On the Saturday morning Billy had been watching the weather forecast with some concern. The Bureau was forecasting a very large and violent storm approaching from the North East. Sure enough looking in that direction a huge mass of very black storm clouds was building up. The flowers were almost finished although there was one more good picking that would end the season, which had already been quite rewarding. Billy went for a tour of the garden and hothouses until he located Phil who was also looking with some dismay at the storm. Billy suggested that

Phil quickly round up any of his regulars and casuals as he could find in a hurry. He himself set out to arrange machinery and packing trays, and locate Jeffery and the tractors ready for the fray.

As the crew members arrived Billy set them on cutting the remaining flowers. He told them to pick everything they could find and load them onto the trays to be sorted out later. Just cut as many as you can and get them off the ground. They laid them out on the tray of the tailor and carryall and in the van. Everyone was magnificent. They worked like mad things to save what they could and parked the trailers in the big barn. When Phil returned Billy said they needed lots of buckets to hold enough water to keep the blooms fresh for a day or two. Then he had a bit of a brain storm saying, "Phil, remember when you were running sheep you had some long metal troughs to feed and water them. I don't suppose you still have them and will they hold water. If they do we can fill them with flowers and wheel them into the barns?

"Yes, Billy I certainly do. I nearly sold them with the sheep but held onto them at the last minute. Hey mate remember all the sundry odds and ends from the clearing sale when we got the tractor, well I reckon there were some among them. The carrier would just have dumped them in the cart shed with all the other stuff and I haven't had time to go through it all. You have a load in the van so you can take that over to the yard, I'll meet you there. As soon as Billy and a couple of helpers arrived in the yard they quickly went through the cart sheds and found three sheep troughs, which they started to fill with flowers and just enough water for them to get a drink or two. Jeffery followed them into the yard with the new tractor and the large trailer full of flowers. Careful handling was needed of course but time was the essence as the flowers were rehoused. As soon as each trough was filled it was wheeled safely into the shed. Most of the flowers were in the shed and the remainder covered with a tarpaulin when there was a horrendous explosion followed up with a string of others and gynormous flashes of continuous lightning bolts streaking up to the clouds and out to the horizon in every direction. All that was followed with a series of bangs and crashes as it suddenly broke out into a massive hailstorm. They called it hail but it was in fact frozen lumps of Ice some as big a tennis balls with normal hail stones as well. The peak of the storm only lasted a few minutes but how much damage would there be? It then settled in to become a heavy down pour turning the ground into a quagmire in seconds. All the flowers were saved, then Billy remembered the glass houses. He shouted to Phil and Jeff. "Hey! You two jump into the van quickly we need to check the greenhouses for damage and broken glass." They threw some tarpaulin sheets in the back in case they were needed and took off like madmen. If there was a lot of broken glass they would need to act quickly to prevent all the heat escaping and chilling the delicate plants growing inside them, and divert the water running down the roofs and washing out the plants. The automatic temperature controls should have kicked in providing extra heat.

When they arrived at the greenhouses they were relieved to find only minor damage due the lumps of Ice. The hail had done very little damage around the garden and most would recover in time. The lumps of ice were limited in number and only seven panes of glass were smashed. Billy shouted to Jeff to take the Austin van back to the farm buildings to get some of the workers to help him load some of the glass sheets left over from the unused end walls whilst he rounded up a large container of putty some scrapers and pliers and any other tools they might need to remove and replace the roof sheets. Jeff loaded the tools some trestles and builder's planks and a step-ladder or two onto the trailer. One of the crew members drove the van carefully and Jeff drove the tractor. They worked in the steady downpour replacing the highest sheets first. The situation was a nightmare because apart from the heavy rain, maybe because of it the water running off the roof was drenching the men as they worked. Billy soon realised the impossibility of doing a good job and told them to just slide the glass roughly into place for the day then they would have a proper go at it after the water dried up in a day or two. The job was quite easy because the broken sheets once removed left a channel to slide the replacement into position in a soggy bed of putty. The putty was just a gluggy mess, but it stopped most of the water from entering The total loss was only very minimal due to early action with the picking and packing. Maybe some of the flowers would not open but most would respond to a good soaking in sunshine over the next day or two.

Once all the tools had been dried and replaced in the store, Billy called out to the troops, "Ok you mob, curry on the house to warm you up again."

Next day, as soon as the sun warmed the yard, Phil and Billy moved the sheep troughs out into the warmth. The troughs had a pair of iron wheels at one end and two metal feet at the other, so they slid a fork handle through the overhead frame, and they each held an end of it so they could lift the legs off the ground and wheel the trough out into the sunshine. The yard was enclosed for the most part reducing wind velocity and allowing the yard to heat up quite quickly in the sun. Phil commented on the weather saying, "We'll need to keep a good lookout for any showers and wheel them back inside in a hurry, and as soon as the sun goes down tonight they will all have to be wheeled back inside to help keep them warm and dry." It was amazing to see how the flowers responded to a bit of sunshine and loving care. Twice each day two of Phil's ladies selected blooms both for the market and the café. Only very few of them were not responding and would need to be discarded, with the rest quickly becoming saleable. After the storm the market became insatiable and Phil was swamped with florists as well as the retail trade in the shop. All things considered the flower growing exercise had proved a winner and it was decided to repeat it the next year. Phil still had a quantity of bulbs in cold store ready to try the winter flowering. He had experimented with planting dates and temperature control and was set to have a go with fingers and toes crossed for good luck. He'll probably need it thought Billy.

Fortunately the café and restaurant seemed to be able to cope with most of their gardening mistakes. A great deal of garden produce is normally thrown away from commercial gardens due to miss shapes, surface markings, and transit damage but most of the rest is perfectly good and usable, in house, if not for resale. Many of Billy's take-away menus were built up around a solid base of vegetables, many of which would normally be thrown away for cosmetic reasons, with meats and proteins added along with an assortment of herbs and spices. This meant that the kitchens had an insatiable need for certain types of vegetables, particularly root and stalk vegetables. The stir-fries for example often used the stalks of leaf vegetables which were normally thrown away during preparation. Fickle housewives and professional cooks will not use bent carrots and oddly shaped cauliflowers etc, whereas Billy and his staff not only used them, he had a copious supply of them rescued from Phillip's grading tables at no cost to the cafe. Just a point, bent carrots taste exactly the same as straight carrots.

Phillip, Jeffery and Billy had another engineering project to sort out at their leisure. The old potato digger needed to be modified with smaller mesh on the conveyors and less shaking to harvest the bulbs at the end of the season. Where the soil was quite sandy it worked really well providing the forward travel was minimised but the engine speed kept normal. This allowed as much time as possible for the crop to break up and separate the bulbs from the dirt. There was still going to be a considerable amount of hand sorting as the bulbs dried off, but far less than digging by hand. Once their own crop of bulbs had been dealt with Billy promised to take the digger over to Spalding to harvest Greg's crop. He would be able to handle the sorting once the bulbs were stored in his shed and once the digging was underway they had plenty of willing helpers to sort out the bulbs from the dirt and rubbish.

Before the trip to Spalding, Billy got together with Jeff to work on a new Idea for harvesting the bulbs. They fitted a rectangular frame vertically to the three point linkage of the tractor with a blade, a worn out blade from the potato digger, welded across the lower end and a row of tines, made from the broken bars of the potato digger welded onto the rear edge, rising upwards to lift the bulbs above the surface of the soil. Because the bulbs, unlike potatoes, were sitting almost on top of the ground and therefore needed very little effort to surface them ready for sorting. They were able to travel much quicker than with the digger and in fact the machine made a, much improved, job when travelling quite quickly.

Jeff was duly despatched with one of their most experienced ladies taking both machines on the tandem trailer. The soils in the Spalding area and surrounds are completely different to any others in England, being a type of peat moss composted from the swamps before draining. Billy thought that either of his machines would work well in the peat and that is how it turned out.

Chapter Seven

However, whilst all the drama was going on in the market garden Melissa was getting on with producing a "son" and heir for Billy and herself. Melissa was enjoying a dream pregnancy and was keeping very well. Billy had a fair amount of difficulty keeping her away from the café but she insisted in doing as much as she could to keep fit but was careful not to overdo it.

Granny Elizabeth had recently moved in to Melissa's old room at Alison and Fred's home to reduce the amount of travelling. This meant that she and Alison could spend lots of time attending to Melissa's needs and mollycoddling her, a fair bit.

A retired couple had offered to lease Granny Elizabeth's home fully furnished because they had just returned from overseas Foreign Service in Kenya. They were both keen gardeners and promised to look after the gardens as well as the house. With all the carry-on you'd think that Alison and Gran were expecting as well as Melissa. Fred had completed the redecorations ready for the nursery and the whole family was spending much of their time at the farm. There was always something that needed doing, or something that needed sorting out so Fred was fully occupied in his spare time whilst his family were billing and cooing over Melissa. Oh my, can you even begin to imagine what it will be like when they actually have a real live baby to fuss over, be it a boy or a girl, as well. as Melissa. Billy was amazed as to how much family support was being shared across himself and his beloved Mel. He had spent all his early life being treated as trash, despised and ridiculed by his family members who should have been looking out for him, supporting and encouraging him to go on to bigger and better things.

Fred was still working more or less full time, but sometimes he was held up with the weather or material shortage Anywhere a useful pair of hands was needed Fred was there and had time to fill in. He was very useful around the garden, the café and the houses. He was constantly repainting and repairing and helping around generally. Billy offered to employ him on a full time basis if ever he wanted a change of scene.

Summer was almost over and the birth of baby Riley was imminent in line with both Mel and Billy's birth dates. Mel had stopped working in the kitchen but still turned up occasionally to keep a watchful eye on the proceedings. The café and the restaurant had first-rate approval from the customers and clientele, but Billy and Melissa were both aware that it would only take one slip to ruin their reputation especially among the lorry drivers who, whilst they were sole operators, had a great relationship with other drivers. They had a weekly magazine called "HEADLIGHT" which kept them up with all the latest trends and gadgets, as well as all the gossip. In his early days at the café, Billy had subscribed to the Headlight and also ran a decent advertisement in each issue. This kept the café in the 'Headlight' so to speak, and the truckers appreciated his interaction and support.

Then it finally happened, in spite of Alison and Granny's constant observations and attendance Melissa was alone in the house when all hell broke loose. First she received a massive labour pain and her waters broke. She had had no early signs that the birth was imminent but time and tide wait for no-one, neither do babies. Fred who had been pottering around the yard sorting out little problems went inside to make a cup of tea for himself and Mel but he found her doubled up on the floor in agony. He grabbed the phone and rang for an ambulance to attend urgently which they did, although it took quite a little while to appear He then made Melissa as comfortable as he could then checked her condition. The baby's head was already appearing and would surely pop out with the next contraction or two. By the time that the ambulance man had a look the baby was halfway out and needing very little assistance from anyone. Fred supported the head whilst Mel let out another scream and the baby popped out. This baby sure was in a great hurry to get into the swing of things and of course it was a boy. The ambulance crew thought that, since Melissa had managed a home birth maybe she should have a home recovery. There was no sign of haemorrhaging or any other problems so as soon as Melissa felt ready they with Fred's help of course carried Mel and the baby upstairs to the nursery and telephoned for the district nurse to attend. The ambulance departed after making sure that Fred was in control and the baby was bathed and settled. Just before the nurse arrived the girls returned to the farm after that all-important shopping spree and tea drinking ceremony to see the exultant Fred in charge of the nursery and helping Melissa to feed the baby. He had the change table all set up for the inevitable eruptions at the rear end of the baby. Nappies were laid out on the warming rack, towels carefully folded at the ready, enamelled bowl, talcum powder you name it, it was all there ready for the next phase. Both women were astounded. Never before had Fred showed any sign of real domesticity. He turned as they walked into the room and asked, "Who needs doctors or midwives any way?

Soon, the astounded ladies found their

tongues and started asking questions so Fred left them to it and retired to the kitchen to organise tea and buns for everyone, remembering of course to telephone the café where he hoped to locate Billy. Billy was out in the market garden with Phil but he was soon alerted and running in the back way to join the ladies upstairs. They screamed at him and sent him away to get cleaned up before they would even let him look at his son let alone pick him up for a cuddle. He desperately needed to cuddle both Melissa and his new son also Alison and granny Elizabeth would need to be pampered, but all that was going to have to wait until he was sterile and dressed. He carried the kitchen scales up to the nursery laid a clean napkin on the tray and lowered the baby onto them to be weighed. "Only seven pounds and fourteen ounces," He called out. Is that the best you could manage my love? Not even eight pounds so we'd better get him on to some Yorkshire puddings straight away. There was a massive outcry from the women folk, but only in jest. Melissa was exhausted but she needed some huge cuddles from Billy before she could rest. The telephone got a huge workout and soon everyone had been notified and the whole place was pure bedlam with well- wishers everywhere. Some were coming, some going, some were telephoning, some brewing tea, and others drinking it. Billy decided that discretion was the better part of valour so he retreated with Phil and a wallet full of pound notes, to the nearest watering hole to wet the baby's head. They collected a few bottles of good quality champagne to take back home along with a crate of beer and a carton of mixed bottles of sherry and Port for the ladies and other friends.

Once all their glasses were filled Phillip stood up to announce a toast, "The toast is, 'Here's to Mathew Riley,' and may all the good fortune in the world be his."

The next link in the chain would have to be a huge party at the restaurant. Weekends were booked out well ahead of time now as the reputation of the restaurant was becoming legendary so it was decided to set the party for a Friday evening after the first full week to give Melissa and the baby time to recover and settle down. Granny Elizabeth put her foot down, demanding more time was needed to bake and decorate another fabulous cake, with Billy's assistance, of course. As a result the party was to be delayed until the following week and Billy telephoned his friends at 'Headlight' magazine to announce the birth of his baby boy and the details of the party to their lorry driver associates.

At the café the next day everyone wanted to shake Billy's hand and congratulate him on his prowess but, as he pointed out to them all, that he actually had very little input in the matter and Melissa had earned all the accolades not him. Billy put a call through to Maude at her home that night telling her that she was now Aunty Maude. Maude, as you can imagine was delighted, over the moon in fact and vowed to travel down in time for the celebrations. She stated that Richard would be equally thrilled and would be coming with her to share the driving. Billy said there would be a bedroom awaiting their arrival so they could select their most comfortable time to drive down, day or night. Maude and Richard packed their bags in plenty of time to allow them to set off immediately after work on the Thursday evening having arranged to have a well earned day off work on the Friday. It was a long drive so they stopped for a break at the 24hr service station south of Sheffield. After a short rest and the usual cup of tea and a sandwich they set off again and arrived at the farmhouse shortly after 10pm.

As soon as they had taken their cases into the house and shared hugs and kisses by way of greetings, Maude held Billy's hands and said, "Guess what Billy, Richard has asked me to marry him and I've accepted. Like you and Mel it will be an autumn wedding. We are planning to be married in the first week of November. Actual date yet to be sorted but we will ring you as soon as we know and hopefully you can come up for the big day. We would assume the café can manage without you for a weekend."

Just then Mel walked into the room with little Mathew in her arms. "Oh my goodness, isn't he tiny? Can I have a cuddle?" Maude asked.

Melissa replied, "I thought that was what you came for, and Mathew won't mind one little bit. He's already a lady's man and laps it all up with glee. Billy and Vanessa walked in at that moment straight from the roadhouse. Billy took Mathew for a quick cuddle then headed to the shower. After his ablutions Billy enjoyed a cup of coffee and lots more kisses and cuddles all round then headed off to bed. This had been a very long day and tomorrow would be even worse. He had to start at 6am to take over from the night crew and organise breakfasts for a good many local people as well as the stream of truckies and motorists coming in off the road. The early morning was bedlam but by lunch time the worst was over so Billy left the roadhouse in the capable hands of his staff and headed home, hopefully to get some sleep before the evening events. Only a minor consideration, but Billy was trying very hard to get his head around an amazing discovery. He was having difficulty working out how a tiny little boy like Mathew could monopolise a mob of women and have them all drooling over his every move, but only until he gets big enough to appreciate the adulation, when at about the time that he can start to appreciate all the worship, it ceases to happen. Oh, what a cruel world we live in.

Breakfast routine was busy as usual with everyone bogging in and getting it done. Once the panic settled down Billy went for a chat with Phillip in the big greenhouse. Everything was looking rosy in there as expected. Billy broached the subject of helping college students to improve their chances of employment in the industry. Phillip agreed with him in view of the success of the roadhouse trials and ongoing employment afterwards. The results had been very gratifying and maybe worth trying in the garden. A quick phone call to Mr. Jones, the principal of the college proved very satisfactory. He had given the matter of students becoming involved with the market garden a good deal of consideration since Billy had first mentioned it, with the result that he was prepared to discuss the deal with the students providing, as before, the college insured the pupil against accidental injury and some indemnity against lasting damage. The parents would be required to sign a release document to cover the college and market garden as well as the student. As before the experiment went quite well with both Jeffery and Phillip accepting the role of tutor. The experiment began cautiously with only two students and quickly extending to six. Their behaviour was strictly controlled and the scheme seemed to be a great benefit to all the parties involved.

Once the student participation settled down and began to run itself Billy began to consider other options for training schools within the organization. For some time he had been thinking about a new government incentive to get handicapped people off dependency and handouts and out into the real workforce. The deal was. of necessity, extremely complex with many regulations, conditions and safeguards. But what the heck, with Melissa back on deck and almost unlimited baby watching by Elizabeth and Alison available, Billy set the wheels in motion. He realised that there were many classes of disability, even just in the physical sense, without getting into the mentally handicapped as well. There were a number of jobs that a handicapped person could carry out successfully around the garden and packing sheds once trained and catered for. To assist these sorts of people, not the least of these would be wheelchair accessibility and there would need to be some, and maybe quite a lot of infra-structural changes to toileting facilities. He made some initial enquiries to the social security department then sat back to watch the fun.

In due course the departments involved got on board. Initially telephoning to set up meetings between the two groups then the big day arrived. Billy arranged to be off shift for a day or two so that he could give this idea his full attention and Melissa joined in as much as possible. Day one was just a look and see for the officials and delivering miles of paperwork to arrange the necessary authorities. Both Billy and Melissa were both blown away by the amount of assistance available. They initially expected most, if not all, the expenses would have to come from their own pockets

but this was not so. The various government departments appeared to have vast amounts of finance to make the project possible. They moved around the garden and more especially the farm buildings to assess the infrastructure needed to make the scheme work. Quite a lot of positions were immediately available for certain candidates but others needed more in depth analysing to make sure that the government funds were well spent with the maximum return. They explained that the wages of the participants would be subsidised to minimise out of pocket costs for the garden. Depending on the levels of handicap, most of the subsidies were quite generous as well. The scheme also worked on a numbers game. It appeared that the more handicapped persons employed the more compensation could be achieved. There was a cut-off limit whereby, if they could manage a greater percentage of handicapped persons compared to normal workers the compensation increased substantially. Billy asked the officials to submit a plan and a list of possible persons from the local area who would benefit from such a scheme. He was truly amazed at the numbers available. Some of the welfare recipients were only mildly afflicted where-as others quite drastically disabled. A few of the listed persons could and were accommodated immediately without any changes to the infrastructure at all. If the scheme could be successfully set up it would greatly improve their seasonal shortages of labour both in the garden and to a lesser degree the café. He was looking forward to interviewing the candidates for suitability. There would need to be a large input by himself and Melissa as well as Phillip and Jeffrey, not just initially but in an on-going role.

Melissa was by now taking the load off Billy by collating all the daily dockets and sundry bookwork this of course included the vital, wages books. They needed to run two current wages books, One for the roadhouse, and a separate one for the market garden. This alone used up a lot of time but Melissa was very competent at the job and she could do most of the bookwork at home in the library where she had set up a comfortable office. Not forgetting of course, lots of 'Help' from Mathew who was now beginning to crawl around the room. Fred had resurrected the old antique wooden play pen that he located in the attics to limit his area of destruction. The worst part of the recycling of the play pen was to remove all the existing paint as it would almost certainly be contaminated with lead. Mathew had been a wonderful baby. He seemed to realise that his Mum had other duties on her agenda and behaved extremely well, and of course he had his Grannies as back up crew.

With Melissa keeping the daily bookwork up to scratch Billy was able to spend a great deal of his time working on the disabled persons set up. Fred and the local building team were working well together alongside the department experts to bring the infrastructure up to scratch. Most able bodied people have no idea how different life can be for anyone with a physical injury or disability and the main problem was that not many if any of them had the same or even similar restrictions in their movements and abilities. Some situations had to be set up so that only one of the staff could work it satisfactorily.

There were so many factors to be considered, not the least of these was access to the work site, toilet facilities and even lunch areas but slowly the project was coming together nicely. As the new employees settled in and began to work within the system there were, of course, many adjustments needed to improve the flow of work but both Billy and Phillip were amazed at how quickly they settled in and became proficient, sometimes excelling over their able bodied co-workers. They seemed to have a knack of extracting far more from the system and increasing total production as well. Billy assumed that because they were privileged to now have employment they were determined to earn that right and prove their worth. Most of the disabled people of both sexes seemed to be able to focus entirely on the job in hand to the exclusion of everything else around them.

Special ride on trolleys were made to allow people without even legs to work in the fields, weeding the crops and even picking strawberries. Some of them actually removed artificial limbs whilst working because they got in the way. They were exceptionally quick at those sort of jobs because they were already much closer to the scene of the action. Less bending meant less back ache, which meant more production. The organisers spent quite a lot of time with Phillip and Billy observing and admiring the adaptations that Billy was designing and asked permission to duplicate them on other projects around the country. Billy thought he ought to hold out for royalties for his designs but he was so glad to be able to help others that he allowed them to copy them free of charge. They brought in some of their engineering staff to draw and sketch the machinery at will. Much of it was specific to Phillip's garden but the engineers were able to adapt and modify some of it to suit other applications. All in all the whole project was proving to be a great success and the social security department staff were astounded with the outcome and promise of even better days ahead. Phillip mentioned to Billy and Melissa over coffee one evening that he thought the able bodied workers had lifted their performance due to the threat of competition from the new crew. This phenomenon appeared to be correct because the slower, lackadaisical, type of worker, really did seem to have lifted their game considerably in fear of their jobs. This attitude definitely improved the relationship among the group and enabled Phil to be more flexible in his daily placement around the garden and packing sheds.

On the whole life was good for the Riley family. Mathew was approaching his first birthday and was beginning to walk although very unsteadily and there were a few tears from time to time when he crashed but he was a very determined young man and nothing was going to stop him in this or any other endeavour Most of their business activities were going along splendidly especially the roadhouse. Poor old Vanessa had been left behind somewhat but her life was quite full. She loved to help out with Mathew and was happy to take a turn at baby-sitting and was now aunty Van or just Van. One morning Billy returned home for a late breakfast and he heard Melissa vomiting in the bathroom. When she settled down and relaxed a bit Billy said to her, "You've been and gone and done it again haven't you. You're always getting yourself knocked up. How many weeks has it been this time."

Melissa grinned at him and replied "Only missed one this time but I'm due again about now so I'm probably only 6 or 7 weeks. I'll ring the doctor today and see what he thinks about it. I'll get some blood test organised as well just to be sure. Working at home here just keeping the books up to date is far less stressful than cooking and running the kitchen at the café. There is quite a lot more work here nowadays with all the handicapped people to attend to. Every week there are lots of claim forms to be addressed to keep the money flowing in. It would help if all our handicapped people had the same problem but as time goes by I am getting to know the people and which category they fit into. Many of them fit quite nicely into two or even more different categories then I have to work out which one best suits us and them The different categories attracted different levels of compensation and assistance so diligence was very important to obtain the maximum amount of money from the authorities for each claimant. How are things at the roadhouse these days, love? Is everyone coping now that we are so busy down there?"

"Yea, you bet, all the staff are pulling their weight and as Phil suggested, having the disabled staff amongst them has really lifted all the others. They know that if they do not perform well enough someone will step into their place. You can't even imagine what it was like that first week I started working in the kitchen. None of the existing staff gave a toss about their boss or the business and worse still their customers. They got the shock of their lives when the axe came down on their heads. Some of them are back with us nowadays but I try to send them into the garden and that often works. They like working there with Phil. rather than the hot kitchen and the no booze rules have changed their attitude and behaviour.

I must get some time soon to run some new ideas past Vanessa. I reckon we can still improve the turnover and profitability. I got on to Michael the other day to get supplies of high quality beef roasts suitable for slicing to extend our range of salad rolls and sandwiches and through summer lots of customers enjoy a salad plate for lunch and dinner with cold meats, salmon and a selection of respectable cheeses.

When Billy finally caught up with Vanessa he put his latest idea forward. He wanted to enclose the front porch and move the doorway out of the café reception area forward to the limit of the building. He pointed out to her that they could then turn the porch into a sizeable shop to catch the customers as they passed through to pay for petrol and food services etc. He wanted to display lots of vegetables, fruits and flowers etc from the market garden. Also they could display and sell loaves of bread, buns and cakes.

Vanessa was happy with the prospect but she was concerned that it would alienate their baker and greengrocer as they would be in direct competition with them. However Billy explained that as far as the baker was concerned it would increase his turnover of bread and other products because most of the goods were to be purchased from him and sold to passing motorists who would not care to stop in town to buy direct from the baker. He did agree that the greengrocer might be a problem but their interaction with him would probably improve as well. Quite a lot of the fruit and vegetable sales would be of products which they themselves did not produce and would need to be bought in from Ernie's place. He was thinking about bananas, oranges, melons, tangerines and other semi tropical fruits like egg plants. Some fruits Ernie did not stock and sell because he would have to buy large quantities, some of which would go to waste but with the roadhouse helping to turn them over anything was possible. Billy had already approached Granny Elizabeth and Alison with the view to allowing them both to work together now Granny was living in Melissa's old room. He suggested that they had a good deal of spare time on their hands and might like to start baking again. He said the café and the new shop would be able to use up as much as they could produce and maybe more. He would set up accounts in the co-op for them to buy wholesale ingredients in the cafes name and they could decide what to bake and when it suited them. He would collect the trays of whatever they turned out each morning and take it to the café. Both Billy and Vanessa could always find excess time to bog in and help the oldies. The extra cash would pay a few bills for them and stock a nest-egg or two, rather than have the oldies sitting around knitting and gossiping. Some of the cakes such as cheese cakes and sponges could be cut up and served in the restaurant as sweets, whilst others would be sold direct to the passing motorists. Even the lorry drivers might pick up a few buns to take with them and pieces of fruit like apples and bananas. There would be no pressure on the ladies with fixed orders every day because they could produce what they wanted and when, as well as how many.

The shop soon became a reality and a second till had to be purchased and extra staff employed to serve across the counter to cope with the huge increase in trade. Phil's cut flowers and potted plants went extremely well and he was battling to keep up the supply. Tomatoes and cucumbers were in big demand along with all the other vegetables. Some of the fuel customers ended up spending more money in the shop than they did for petrol.

As the saying goes, time really does fly and soon it was time for the birth of the latest baby, be it boy or girl. Melissa and the other ladies were determined that it would be a girl this time and they proved to be correct. Once again Mel produced a good sized full term baby and Mathew was delighted even though it was a girl. Elizabeth, after her great Grandmother of course, was a delight to have around and soon made her presence known in every way. She was a demanding little devil but all the nicer for that. The birth event slowed the flow of cakes for a day or two but Billy honed his skills in the roadhouse kitchen to keep up the supply and used the experience to further the education of the kitchen staff. Some of them were always ready to take on new skills and improve their lot. Billy allowed them to continue to produce pies, pastries, and cakes whenever they had spare time during a shift. One girl Beatrice, was extra keen and begged to be allowed to work in the kitchen even in her own time, so Billy encouraged her to do so, provided she didn't impede the normal usage and she kept a list of all she produced so that Melissa knew how much extra to pay her. She turned out a good supply of very saleable pastries and cakes and set herself up for an alternate career in case she ever felt like a change.

Chapter Eight

About that time Maude announced her wedding date. She and Richard had finally got their lives into synch and were looking forward to the big day. They had been offered to turn Maude's digs into a marital home for the time being and that arrangement suited everyone. Billy and Melissa needed to do some serious juggling if they were to attend the ceremony. The main problem was, "Do they take the babies or leave them with their Grandmothers". Maude was keen to get her hands on the little blighters again but that was going to have to wait a while. Melissa opted to leave the babies, stay overnight, and return the next day. The happy couple were getting married in a nice Methodist chapel near their new home. Maude was extremely clever at baking and decorating cakes which she sold as a hobby to all her friends and workmates so she opted to bake the cake and decorate it herself. Maude even made all the decorations instead of buying them in and the result was quite magnificent.

When Billy and Melissa arrived at the flat Billy asked if Joe had been invited to the event and Maude informed him that he definitely had not and there was never any chance that he would be, unless he found out where the ceremony was to be held and had the audacity to turn up at the chapel.

Before going on Maude said I need to tell you that Dad has picked up his life again and changed dramatically. She went on to tell them that he had eventually left the farm contracting business and he'd had to buy a decent cottage to live in. It was close to the other house in the same village so he could start working as a lorry driver for a nearby firm. There was lots of extra work with the firm and Joe soon managed to find a deposit for a neat little tip truck allowing him to go into business on his own alongside his main job. He'd noticed that there was a shortage of small tip trucks in that area to attend to many local deliveries. He obtained a couple of contracts for permanent deliveries and one with the West Riding County Council and that left enough time for him to continue the casual jobs as well.

All this went well but left Joe with a domestic problem. He was always out on the road earning big time and he was never into home duties and the house was a pig sty. Most of his meals he picked up along the way so cooking wasn't a problem. Both of the contract firms he worked with had excellent canteens which provided very cheap nourishing meals whenever he called in.

One of the office girls where he called regularly declared that she remembered him from way back. That was quite true as it transpired, and they had always got on well together for many years so they had a good old natter over lunch. It turned out that the lady had recently lost her loving husband and she'd had to sell her house. She was living in a pretty decrepit old flat whilst looking around for a nice cheap cottage to rent or buy. After meeting her a few times over the next few weeks Joe offered her a job as his live-in house keeper. They arranged to meet up one night after work and Joe took her to see his house, which he had spent a lot of time on recently, cleaning it up to get it looking half decent again. The lady was happy to move in and occupy the spare bedroom but she declared that she would still keep working at the factory as well. She pointed out that the house was far too small to occupy her full time. When they had been living together for some time they decided to get married. They attended a civil ceremony and according to casual observers the union was going well.

Although it was none of his business Billy wished Joe well and hoped he had learnt some lessons by now. Maude was kept informed by a couple of acquaintances how things were going for Joe, both in his business and his personal life, so she realised that her old man had almost certainly heard about her wedding. Joe, and Barbara his new wife, did turn up for the wedding ceremony at the chapel but they sat quietly at the rear of the chapel and left as soon as the bridal party stepped outside. He didn't make any attempt to speak to either of his offspring or get involved with the reception.

The ceremony went well with Maude's workmate Penny acting as Brides Maid and Her boyfriend Frank as Best Man. There was a cosy little hall attached to the chapel which they were able to hire for a reception party. The radiogram from their lodgings and many of their own records provided the music. They had hired a catering group to attend to their guests and the home made cake was the centre of attraction. Some of the guests took down Maude's phone number vowing to ring her next time they needed a special cake for birthdays, Xmas, etc. Once the feast was over the dancing began and went on until very late. They were only a small group but well suited and they all enjoyed a great evening's entertainment. Maude had reserved a nice hotel room for Billy and Melissa so they crashed for the night and were facing a long journey home in the Jaguar in the morning.

The return trip went well with Melissa sharing some of the driving. She loved driving the Jaguar now she was used to it. The car was up to the occasion and purred happily along the highway. Mel asked, "Does this bring back memories for you Billy."

"Oh no, not at all I was sound asleep most of the way the last time. I only remember a few roundabouts."It was only when the tractors slowed down and changed gears to negotiate the roundabouts that I was awakened and went straight back to sleep once the outfit settled down again, We'll stop at the roadhouse south of Sheffield for a meal and tea break. That's the only real memory I have of all the journey. It was interesting to check the difference between that roadhouse and their own. There was no comparison at all. It looked as though it'd had no attention or upgrades since Billy was here last although he only wanted a decent mug of tea on that occasion. The Sheffield trucker's café and even that was a strong exaggeration was such a disappointment. It was grotty, overdue for a new design and décor, and severe updating, to bring it up to scratch. The food was mediocre at best, the service woeful and slapdash but it was the only 24hr. stop for a good many miles in both directions. No wonder the lorry drivers whinged about roadhouses in general and flocked to their place whenever possible. Billy and Mel walked out in disgust without waiting to be served and looked out for a better venue further down the road. They discovered a quaint little roadside café nearby and enjoyed a quality meal in comfort.

It was a pleasant return home where they were swamped with the kids and grandparents. As soon as possible they were both cuddled up in the big shower washing away the weekend detritus. They decided there and then to try for baby number three. When he had time to sit down with Melissa cuddled up beside him he thought about the story Maude had related concerning his father and he was pleased that he was at peace at last. He realised that there would never be any dialogue between himself and his estranged father. Joe had always been unforgiving and dogmatic and he would never change. Billy was just so thankful that Joe controlled himself at Maude's wedding and didn't cause an incident although he must have found it very difficult to behave judging by the tight strained facial expressions, especially when Billy accidentally got too close. Maybe it was for his new wife's sake that he held it all in check and controlled his savage temper and ill feelings.

On the latter part of their journey home Melissa seemed to have something worrying her. Billy was aware of a slight change in the atmosphere in the car and he eventually called a halt to it. By saying, "Ok Mrs. Riley let's have it. I can tell something's bothering you so spit it out. Get it off your chest, and you'll feel a lot better."

Melissa looked quite guilty and admitted that there was something on her mind. She began with, "Well its nothing much really, but I'm sick of you coming up with all the crazy ideas to make more money in the café. That wouldn't be too bad but you are nearly always right, they nearly always work out well. So, I have decided to join in and give it a go as well."

"OK Einstein, what have you come up with? I hope it won't break the bank."

"No silly, it won't do that and what's more it won't cost us a single penny, ever, and the money will keep rolling in forever without us doing anything at all except count it. You see my love whilst you were busy in the little boy's room at the trucking café I got to talking to a man who was servicing that music thingy in the corner of the café. I think it's called a jukebox. Anyway, the company that owns it, will install it free of charge and we get to share in the takings. All we have to do is provide a suitable power point in the wall and pay for the electricity that it uses. They don't use a great deal of power anyway, and the profit margin is good."

"That all sounds to be too good to believe, sweetheart, are you quite sure he wasn't just having you on,"

"Oh yes there you go again. I'm just a silly old woman, easily taken in by a smart arsed salesman. Well here you are have a read of this, then ring the company and check for yourself, Mr. Smarty Pants. You'll see and end up eating your words."

"Whoa Darling I'm not knocking the idea just being a little cautious, that's all. When we get back home I'll check it out for you. Have you decided where we can put it in the café or the restaurant."

"Oh yes that's the easy bit. That awkward corner, the one near the rear door. We tried putting a small table in there if you remember but the chairs kept blocking the access to the doorway. I'm quite sure that there is a power point close to the floor in the corner of the wall because we use it for the vacuum cleaner and floor scrubber. But, listen, Billy my love, that isn't the end of my ideas. The salesman said that his company can easily install a couple of those one -armed bandits as they are called and we can make pots of money from them as well. They could fit onto the wall just inside the end of the counter."

Billy was blown away by his clever wife and decided to enquire about it all, first thing in the morning but firstly they would need to run the ideas past Vanessa for her approval. He believed that they would need to get permission from the council as well. They already had permission from the council to provide music in the restaurant so extending it into the café shouldn't be a problem and he had heard that some of the pubs and hotels around the area, had been granted permission to install the poker machines, or one -armed bandits as they are aptly named.

It was so good to be back home even though they were only away for one night. First thing next morning Billy wandered down to the market garden to try and catch up with Phil. Each and every member of their work force greeted him warmly and asked how the trip had gone. When he finally found Phil he received a big surprise. Their big Ferguson tractor was busy at work with a new three furrow plough on the back, ripping up a large area of pasture but not on their side of the fence. It was on Phil's side of the dividing wall with about twenty acres ahead of it. Jeff must have had a very early start and the tractor was running nicely, on what was close to its maximum load. It looked a bit queer to anyone uninitiated with farming because the right hand wheels were running in the previous furrow and the tractor tilted heavily to one side. As Billy approached the tractor slowed to a stop and greetings were exchanged and Jeff asked, "Well boss, what do you think about this have I got it set about right do you reckon?"

Heck, yes, it looks great, but what the heck are you doing in this field.

"Ah yes, simple really, boss. Phil has sold his

breeding ewes and wants us to plough and crop this low-lying ground with spuds and roots for the first year then general market gardening for the subsequent years. Here he comes now he can tell you himself and I'll get on with it."

"Hey there Phil, what's happening around here today. I only sneak off for a quick weekend and this is what I come back to." Said Billy

"Yeah, sorry about that mate, meant to tell you last week but I reckoned you'd be pleased anyway. We have plenty of scope to sell root vegetables, like carrots, parsnips, turnips, etc, and there seems to be an insatiable market for spuds and winter greens so I got rid of my sheep and started digging up this field for now. It should grow a good profitable crop for this year and I'll decide what and when to attack the other two. We have to be careful not to over extend ourselves and not be able to manage the crops well enough."

Billy answered Phil making the comment that he was delighted and had been looking over that wall since the very beginning and if the results in the little fields were repeated they would make a lot of money, weather permitting. because these new fields were slightly higher up the hill and did not flood in the last big flood Billy glanced at his watch and remembered his promise to Melissa about the jukebox. He managed to put a call through to the sales manager of Royston's Music and Entertainments in Birmingham.

The manager explained to Billy that the salesman had put aside the latest and biggest of their machines, and they were not keen to install it into an unknown and untried venue. They were hoping to install it in a high traffic area such as a seaside resort or other tourist oriented site. This machine because of its cost and size was going into a busy site somewhere, preferably one where they already had a smaller machine and needed to upgrade it. Billy hoped he had convinced the man of the need for this particular machine but the man said if it did not prove viable immediately they would need to remove it quickly and, replace it with one of their older, smaller models. Finally a temporary truce was agreed on and they promised early delivery. They only had one of these expensive machines in stock at that moment and they needed to get it out working as soon as possible to begin to recoup their capital outlay.

Billy was assisting in the kitchen mid-morning the following day when the van arrived, much to his surprise, and two men alighted from the cabin. The driver was the installer that Melissa had chatted with in the roadside café. The passenger walked over quickly and introduced himself as the manager of Royston's amusements and music. They left the driver to open the van and set up the trolley and prepare for unloading the jukebox, whilst the manager walked with Billy into the café. The manager was still not certain that this was the ideal placement for the latest machine or any machine at all. They already had machines in smaller roadside cafes with only marginal returns, including the one near Sheffield.

Billy showed the manager the selected position for the jukebox which proved to be highly satisfactory. He then asked Billy how many hours a week he anticipated it would be in use and roughly how many patrons would attend the café each day.

Billy told him, much to his amazement, that the café was always open 24 hrs. per, day and 7 days per, week with a constant stream of patrons most of the time, even throughout the night . The manager settled down very quickly, and assisted in the installation, and commissioning, of the machine. He explained all the workings and he shoved a few coins in the slot and invited Billy to select three songs, which he did. He adjusted the volume control and locked it in place to prevent tampering by clients and they were in business. He got out some documents that he needed to get signed then prepared to leave but Billy had another trick up his sleeve.

Billy asked George about the poker machines which they also had on board. He asked, "George, are those poker machines all spoken for or can we have them as well as the jukebox."

George scratched his near bald head and looked at his assistant who said, "They are ordered and expected to be delivered this week sometime, but not necessarily today and we have quite a number of each in stock to satisfy the original order, so if you have somewhere suitable to install them you can have them now if you want them. How many have you got room for, show me?"

"Come over here, next to the end of this counter between it and the outer wall. We can easily move these shelves which we don't really need here now that the shop next door is working well and I reckon you might fit three or four along this wall. There are only two power points here but we can soon get the local sparky in here and fix that. I spotted some very nice padded stools in the second hand shop the other day to keep the punters comfortable whilst they squander their money."

The salesman measured the available space declaring that there was indeed plenty of room for four machines so Billy asked him to start installing them whilst he organised the stools and rang the electrician who thought he could be there before the men departed back home to Birmingham. It was relatively easy to install 2 more power points below the poker machines and they were in business. The stools were interlocked into two pairs to minimise movement and traffic jams. Much to everyone's amazement the jukebox machine was being used before the sales crew departed. The salesman said he would call regularly but he showed them how to open the back of each machine and empty the cash before it jammed the works. All of the machines needed to be emptied regularly because the usage was very much higher than expected especially the jukebox which seemed to run continuously day and night. Melissa took great delight in opening the jukebox and retrieving all the coins therein. It was her daily job of course to keep the records of monies taken out and balance the books. The machines all had counters installed so she always had a check point to reckon their take. So there they were, another day stuffed up but hopefully a good profitable outcome thanks to Melissa. Billy was due to be in the kitchen that night so he headed for the shower and bed. Hopefully his kids would allow him a little peaceful sleep.

The following spring Billy and Melissa received a phone call from his sister Maude telling him that she and Richard were happily expecting a baby at last, but not too soon.

It was due in what appeared to be a family baby month or two, actually, August or early September but as yet no idea of the sex. Maude then dropped a bit of a bomb shell. They had been to a show at the Royal Hall and on the way out they had bumped into Joe and Barbara on the steps down from the front entrance. After a few uncomfortable moments Joe had asked Maude, "Now then Lass how are you keeping. This is your husband Richard isn't it. We, Barbara and me, have been hoping to bump into you both and clear the air, so to speak."

"Yes Dad we've both felt that way and we were a bit disappointed when you left our wedding in such a hurry and missed out on the reception, Of course we had our Billy and Melissa with us that day and it would have been extremely awkward for everyone, but this is much better. I understand that the two of you are now married and living happily in Stavely village."

"Aye well lass, it's good to catch up with you both, did you enjoy the show."

"Yes it was magnificent, wasn't, it especially the grand finale."

"I suppose, you must have heard, I've got my own lorry now and a couple of excellent contracts that mostly keep me busy and plenty of casual loads as well. We are doing very nicely and Barbara still runs the office at Yorkshire stock foods. She looks after all my book work as well. She's a right good hand is Barbara aren't you love?"

"Aye well, you keep saying that Joe so there must be some truth in it. Hello to you both, nice to meet you officially, like. I hope you are both keeping well. I understand you are both gainfully employed and doing well."

Maude and Richard congratulated them on their success in business and their marriage. They all bade each other goodnight and went their separate ways. Maude turned to Richard saying, "That was a nice surprise, I'm so glad that Dad has got his life together again and maybe we can be friends with him. He never, ever belted me, nor even hit me so I can stand back from all that, even though it caused my mother's death. I can try to forgive him, for that, but it will take time to heal completely, if at all. With our Billy it's a different scenario, because he will never forgive the old sod no matter what he does in the future. My old man never apologises to anybody, or for anything, and if you could get him to talk about what he did to our Billy he will still believe that he got his due deserts, and as his father he was entitled to be as brutal as he felt like at that time. Apparently he damaged Billy's kidneys quite badly because he was urinating blood for more than a week after he arrived in Haversby. His boss-cum-landlady was getting very worried about it. She had been a fully trained hospital nurse prior to inheriting the roadhouse from her Grandparents and knew more or less what was going on with Billy's kidney's. She had reluctantly decided to seek full medical assistance at the hospital when it finally cleared up itself , without any interference If Billy had needed to be hospitalised his past history would have been revealed and he would have been dragged back to Yorkshire and who knows what punishments and further brutalities. Only time will tell us if there is any permanent damage to his kidneys and other organs but for now he seems fit enough."

About a year or so later Melissa apprehended Billy when he rushed home for a quick lunch before heading out to the garden, she showed him a cutting from the Yorkshire Evening post dated some week or two ago. Once he had time to read and absorb the details, she asked, "What do you think about that Billy my love?"

"To tell you the truth sweetheart, it doesn't surprise me at all. As we saw when we called in there. What!!! More than a year ago now, wasn't it? The whole place was a disaster and probably running at a loss then. It would have been mainly fuel sales, especially at night when all the other sites were shut that was keeping it afloat. I reckon they're pretty optimistic with their pricing. I wouldn't mind having a look at their books. Wages alone would be killing them unless they have improved it since we were there. Hey, my darling, are you suggesting that we buy it and run the two from here."

"Well I do need to get you out from under my feet and out of my bed. We've already got three of the little blighters under foot and another one on the way. Melissa had delivered another baby girl about one year after baby

Elizabeth who she named Marion and she was now almost one year old."

"How did you manage that one my love, are you blaming me again. I've already been blamed for the other three now you're trying to hang another one on the chart."

"Ok I'm not really sure yet but you know what I'm like. I'm really sick of you finding out before me, so this time I've been checking every date and I reckon it's already happening."

"So your kicking me out to Sheffield for a week or two is that the score."

"Don't be silly my love it takes a lot longer than that."

"Ok I'll ring the agent and see how the land lies. As far as I'm concerned it is only worth the land value. There will be little or no good will attached and most of the plant is knackered or obsolete, even the petrol pumps." I was just wondering about our Maude, you've seen how clever she is with cake making and decorating and, boy, oh, boy can she cook and present a great roast dinner. Our income here is killing us with kindness and filling the inland revenue coffers with gold so we need to invest some capital off site and a project like this could come in very handy with plenty of capital growth as well."

"Right you are then my lovely, you get on and get me another son or two and I'll get us another roadhouse or two. How does that sit on your shoulders? Just remember that it was you're idea and we both know what happened the last time your little brain spat out some ideas." Commented Billy.

"There you go again Mr. Smarty pants, trying to knock me down even though the last lot turned out to be a gold mine that is still producing gold, lots of it. Don't you forget Billy Boy I do all the books for that project and others so I know how good it is. Will you ask Vanessa to join in or do you want to go it alone."

"Good point love, we have a different agenda to Vanessa we have to house all these kids you keep producing and eventually find them jobs or careers. I will make an appointment to see the bank manager and have a talk with Vanessa. If she wants to be involved that will suit me but if not I will look at going alone, with my clever wife of course. Our accountant might have some suggestions about the best way of doing it now Mathew is getting old enough to be a partner. I know it is a long way off but these things need to be factored in sooner rather than later.

The next morning Billy called the bank for an appointment to see the manager. The receptionist suggested 1.00 pm might suit her boss if that was acceptable to Billy, which it was. The manager Jeffrey welcomed Billy into his office and mildly berated him for staying away so long. Billy pointed out to him that it was a measure of his business success that meant he'd had no call, nor any time to bother Jeffrey. Jeffrey asked what then had prompted this visit because before Billy arrived he had checked the accounts and was amazed how plush they were, both his and Melissa's. The various roadhouse and garden accounts were also well plumped up. Billy explained about the Sheffield roadhouse and how it might be acquired.

Jeffrey was your typical bank manager, extremely cautious and suggested that he would be able to set everything in motion provided the figures lined up well. As Jeffrey said, "Billy you and you alone have done this sort of deal before and all on your own so I have every confidence that you can pull it off. Have you discussed it with Vanessa yet. She might be in a position to go along with you and minimise your borrowings."

"No not yet Jeffery that is my next port of call but I don't want to overload Vanessa at her age. Also I have an appointment this afternoon with Ronald Rhodes who will need to be involved sooner rather than later."

"Ok then William away you go and good luck. Remember to keep in touch so I can and will help you if needed. So, I'll say good afternoon for now and look forward to future discussions on the project. Just make sure that you get every detail down on paper and get it signed."

"Thank you for your time Jeffrey, I'm sure something will eventuate but only if the figures add up. They are asking far too much for the place at the moment but they had to start somewhere. Good afternoon to you Sir, I'll be in touch in a few days."

The next stop had to be Vanessa who happened to be off duty at that time. Over a nice cup of coffee, they discussed the possible purchase of the Sheffield place and Vanessa was quite sympathetic to their cause but was not insisting in being a part of the deal, although she was interested in jointly purchasing the real estate if it could be separated from the business. She said, "Well there you are then, Billy, the entrepreneur. Yes mate joint land owner if you can manage to steal it, I'm in if not it's all yours."

Next port of call was Billy's accountant Ronald Rhodes. He, typical of his calling, was very cautious but he said he could do with a day out and a ride in Billy's latest Jaguar motorcar. As a result, Billy called the agent in Sheffield to arrange a suitable day unless it had already been sold. The agent was quite despondent about the sale as they had not had any enquiry to date. He told Billy that the elderly gentleman who owned the place was long overdue to retire and his health was going downhill fast, hence the lack of attention to the décor etc, Billy had not realised that the advert Melissa had seen was not the first one it had been on offer for more than five or six months with no interest. He managed to organise a day when both he and Melissa could be spared as well as his accountant Ronald Rhodes. These days Melissa was very busy and although she was no longer working full time in the kitchen, her other duties kept her on the trot, so time off had to be carefully arranged. Naturally, baby sitters and kid organisers was no problem with Grannies constantly around, baking cakes and pastries. In view of the fact that Alison and Elizabeth were spending much of their time at the farm house Billy had the gas oven pulled out and replaced it with the latest gas cooking range. It was a large commercial range with 8 cook-tops and three separate ovens all in stainless steel so it was easy to keep clean.

Chapter Nine

Fortunately they had chosen a lovely sunny day for the trip to Sheffield and Fred had organised his schedule so he could have a good look at the buildings and décor, because Billy and Melissa were likely to call on his expertise in the remodelling. Fred was slowing down and even thinking about retiring so this could possibly his last enterprise of any magnitude. So off they went with Ronald and Fred getting to know one another in the rear seats and Billy initially driving with Melissa beside him. He had worked out that it was 100miles each way so they should be there around time for morning tea break. Billy shouted them all to a nice tea break at the roadside café where Billy and Mel had called after Maude's wedding. He thought initially that they ought to have completed the journey to the roadhouse and refreshed themselves there to see if it had improved.

When they arrived at the roadhouse they were introduced to the agent who was handling the sale. He was anxious to move on and he was not really expecting any action that day and he had other appointments which were more likely to result in a sale and profit for himself. Roger Jefferson introduced himself and shook hands with each of them asking, "Which of you is the interested party in purchasing this property, and or, is it the business that you want? Where do you want to start?"

"Billy said, "There are a number of issues to be dealt with in this matter, but if it's going to be so much trouble for you we'll go elsewhere. Maybe your office can assign some other agent to assist us, one who really cares, if not we have other properties and business proposals to look at today and like you, we do not have time to waste. We have travelled over 100 miles to view this property and as you can see from the outside, the place is a tip and should be bulldozed. Inside it is probably just as bad if not worse so if you would like to call your boss we can sort it out quickly and move on"

"No, no, no, Mate I can handle this easily. You've miss-understood me. My office listed this property nearly 6 months ago, and up to .now and no-one has made even the slightest enquiry let alone made an offer. Do you want to make an offer now, or if not, where do you want to go to from here."

"There are many things to look into and assess before we make any offers at all. Are you available to go through all this now. or will you leave it to us to make an assessment before we put forward an offer. I don't see a queue of buyers lined up with their cheque books at the ready."

"Yes, I'm at your disposal. I'll just ring the office to let them know where I'm likely to be for some time."

"Ok that sounds quite positive. Are the current owners on site at the moment and when can we all get together to sort things out."

"They are not available now because they were working all night but later on after we get sorted they will come in and talk to you. Are you seriously interested in making an offer?"

"We came all this way to look at the real estate and buildings, as well as the business, so yes, we are serious provided we can prune the figures to reflect the true value of the building, the plant and any other relevant factors."

"Ok where do you want to start?" Asked Roger demurely.

"Right you are, but let me make you understand where we are. The building and real estate we will value first off. Do you have any breakdown of the figures or will this just be one big guess."

"The owners just wanted to set a single figure and I tried to explain to them that any serious buyer would need to have it broken down or they would just offer a rock bottom price."

"Ok," said Billy do you have any up to date valuations of this place and or similar buildings in the area and an engineer's report on the stability of the buildings."

"A vacant block of land as big as this and positioned as this is valued quite well for development purposes subject to council approval, of course." Said Roger.

"Right you are, you have those values to hand.

Before you go on I must point out as I'm sure you know, if we or anyone else were to try and develop this land the underground fuel tanks of which there must be quite a number will all have to be removed and the holes backfilled and compacted. Add to that the engineer's fees and rezoning costs and this land has little value if any."

"Yes here they are. I got three valuations by independent agents."

"So these prices are for a cleared site ready to build on with council approval to go with them. Let's remember that council approval and rezoning could take up to 18 months and the cost of clearing has to be factored in."

"Sorry chaps I seem to have got your offer mixed up. I believed that you were wanting to buy the place outright as a going concern, not knock it down and develop the site."

"Quite correct but we need to get a true valuation before we can start. Ok, you have paperwork to establish the owner's rights and his or your valuation. Give those to my accountant here and let him tell us what it might be worth.

"So Ronald, let's go through these books and work out a true value. Tell me Roger do you have a rock bottom figure beyond which it will be a non event."

"Yes, Ok here it is. I should not be showing you this at this time but I feel that without it you will back away. This includes all the plant, fittings and fixtures, as well as projected profits for the next two years."

"I realise that fuel sales especially between, say, 6 pm and 8 am will always do well but the cost of keeping the kitchen open is a nightmare because the menus are terrible, the service non-existent and the quality of meals quite atrocious. Even a hungry trucker would not enjoy what they serve up, even in the daytime, let alone at night. We would have to install a complete new kitchen with the latest appliances then re-staff the place to get it back on track. If there is any doubt in your mind I hereby invite you and your clients to visit our roadhouse complex south of Haversby to help you to understand how bad this place is. We will shout you all to a free gourmet meal of your choice should you decide to make the journey."

"So, Billy let's get down to the nitty gritty, What you are saying is, you are not remotely interested in this roadhouse as a going concern are you? You're looking only for a development site am I correct?"

"No that's not correct either Roger. we have prepared a counter offer which my accountant, Ronald, here has worked out based on the figures supplied and Fred here has assessed the approximate time and cost to bring the place up to scratch. You will realise that the kitchen will need to be closed for more than a month at least, maybe two in fact, depending on the availability of the new equipment and whilst repairs are under way. After all who knows what we will find when we start to redevelop the kitchen alone, never mind the rest of it. We will have to be assured of the councils co-operation before we start.

We realise you will have to consult the vendors and see if they are prepared to compromise, meanwhile Fred and I will go upstairs to evaluate repairs and redecorations needed up there, if you don't mind. Then we'll enjoy a nice lunch down the road and return at 2 o'clock. Hopefully, by then, you will have a satisfactory answer for us but unless the upper stories are paved with gold we will not vary our offer very much. Thank you for your time and patience, we do want this café if we can agree on a fair price." Billy shook hands with Roger and moved upstairs with Fred and the others followed.

As they moved off Ronald commented, "I hope I never have to do any business dealings with you Billy, you are a hard man to get along with and you don't miss a single trick."

Billy replied, "Hey Ronald, you've heard some of my story and believe me, some of it is a lot worse than any you've heard. The only break I ever received was at 2 am one cold, rainy night when Vanessa decided that I would possibly be a great investment provided that I lived up to my promises, which I have done 1000 times over and more."

Both the upper stories were very tired and needed a completely new décor. Fortunately both floors already had bathrooms which would need to be gutted and refurbished but that was only to be expected and there was plenty of room in the largest room to install an en suite shower and toilet facility and maybe a walk-in wardrobe. It appeared to have been the living room in days gone by but one of the smaller rooms would suffice in that regard. They had a quick look into the attics but it was impossible to see much because they were full of old furniture and assorted bric-a-brac. Fred was anxious to get in there if the vendors left it all behind because he was sure there would be plenty of renovation work to amuse him in his retirement, once we removed and dumped the junk and clutter, that is.

There were not too many problems areas throughout the upper stories, except for a lot of paint, all new curtains, and floor coverings. If the sale went through there was going to be plenty of work for everyone, however, much of it could wait until the business area on the ground floor was finished. Billy said that he would need a couple of the better bedrooms roughly liveable for his own use initially, then, they could be upgraded later.

Well that was that, into the jaguar and back to the roadside café for a pleasant lunch. Who knew what the afternoon would bring? Time alone would answer that question.

Back at the roadhouse all the introductions were made and Roger asked, "Have you come up with a plan as yet Billy, we really need to increase the price as it is far too low at the moment. My clients need to retire and it will be difficult at your valuation. How much are you prepared to raise your offer."

"As I said before this is a straight business deal and no emotions are to be considered. We have assessed the costs of refitting the property and as I said before we cannot even consider much of a compromise. We have already carried out similar restorations at Haversby and have a very good idea of costs without working out a full and comprehensive budget today. Actually we are very close to the reserve price set by your clients here and we do not want any of the internal fittings and fixtures, they will all have to go under the hammer or in some cases straight to the nearest rubbish dump. They will all have to go. We may have to close the kitchen and café for as much as 1 month or two even to make the refit run much smoother so if there is anything inside that you would like you may take it on change-over day. "Look here I will make you one last offer, as I said there is not much between what you want and what I am prepared to pay so I am happy to split the difference, shake hands on the deal and let our lawyers sort out the final details. To assure you of my goodwill, if we write up and sign the contracts now I will give you a cheque for ten percent of the agreed value and we can all go home. Roger can you finalise this deal ready for signing now and take over by the end of next month. That will give you thirty days to sort out any anomalies. However In view of the extra cash I would like permission to have free access to the upper floors as from Monday morning. If we can get the upper floors habitable by 'D' day it will help us to change over smoothly. I will keep in touch in case you think of any of the goods and chattels that you might want to keep. If Fred here, and myself are on site during the next month I can help you out and even take a hand in the kitchen, from time to time to ease your workload and stress."

So, that was the end of a very stressful day for everyone. There were handshakes all round, Billy wrote out the cheque as promised and they headed off home after snacks at the roadside café. Billy's next task was to write to the editor of Head Light magazine and supply him with a carefully worded statement as to their intentions to refurbish the Sheffield roadhouse and turn it into Billy's Place No. 2 and begin to prepare suitable advertisements ready for the grand reopening.

On the way home there was only minimum chatter between the group but Ronald asked Billy, "Well Billy that went quite well in the end didn't it. I thought they were going to stick out for a fair bit more. I personally reckon you got yourselves a bargain even though it was hard fought. I thought the real estate was worth more than you paid for the whole lot. Are you really going to ditch everything and start again?"

"Oh yes we are going to clear the building and refit all the rooms in time. The petrol pumps and associated equipment outside all has to be updated but the cost will be next to nothing because I have already spoken to the fuel companies about re-equipping all the pumps, advertising signs, both in the yard and out on the approaches to town. The secret to all that, is that, the fuel contracts are all overdue for renewal, and none of the fuel companies will have any hold over the site. I have already canvassed the main companies to tender for the new site and they are all scrambling to get in first. I will only allow two firms to make the final bids and they don't know as yet that they will both have access to the site and mainly at their expense. Provided I sign up for a five year contract they will erect all new signage, new pumps and any ancillary equipment. At the moment Mobil Oil Company and Shell petroleum are favourites, with BP on their heels. Texaco aren't in the running unless they do some quick arithmetic. I expect the winners to move in on takeover day and make a start. They need to keep some of the pumps operating at any one time and they estimated the whole site will be operating within 1 week. Now that I have signed the deal and paid a deposit I can authorise them to work out what equipment they'll need and assemble it ready to go."

Back at the farm the kids all went mad for a while until they had all caught up with their missed kisses and cuddles. After dropping off Ronald the other three settled down for a conference of war. Mel commented, "I can hardly believe we bought that roadhouse with so little haggling and no real arguments. Is it really ours now? Can they back out at the last minute?

Billy replied, "Not unless they have a really good legal team and can find a loophole to crawl through. All four of us have signed and contra signed every document and I honestly believe the old couple were glad to sign in the end. They almost got their reserve price and they will sleep well this night, I feel sure."

As soon as Billy could see his way clear to disappear for a while he went to have a good long chat with his builder friend. Billy asked Adrian, "How is business mate? How much time will you have next month?"

"Ah Billy, that's a leading question, because it depends on what you have on your mind. The way the weather is closing in we'll be held up with a number of projects and we could do with lots of inside jobs to fill in the gaps. So what have you got on your mind this time? I don't suppose you want me to build you a new café somewhere around the place because that would include lots of outdoor work as well."

"Heck mate you must be psychic. You are so close to the mark except that the outside work is already done. I arranged for a quality builder to do that about forty years ago. Now I need you to finish the interior. It's one heck of a big job and if you find it's too much, please just say so."

"Ok where is this castle of yours and when can I see it?"

"Being as tomorrow is Sunday and you don't go to church, how about I pick you up in the Jag first thing and take you for a bit of a ride up country."

"So this will be a mystery tour will it? Why all the secrecy? What's going on in your miniscule brain this time?"Adrian wanted to know.

Billy replied, "I will have to keep it a secret until you agree to do it. That way you won't be able to say no until you have made a sensible decision, and I have picked your brain for what little knowledge it contains. It's quite a long drive so how about I pick you up at 6 o'clock in the morning."

"Right you are then, can I bring Gwen and Allan along as well? They don't get out and around much when I'm busy. Its ages since I took them out for a drive in the country."

"Plenty of room in the motor for them and I'll bring Mathew for a ride with us." Billy answered.

It was just before 6 o'clock when the Jaguar pulled into Adrian's yard and tooted the horn, but they were all ready and eager to be off and Allan ran out and jumped in the back with Mathew. Adrian and Gwen followed more sedately and Gwen wanted to know if they needed anything with them. Billy assured them that all he needed was the three of them, because he had already put in plenty of snacks and nibbles to keep them all contented.

Gwen said "Good morning Billy and you too Mathew. It sounds like this is one heck of a long trip if we need all that sustenance to stay alive until we get there."

Billy replied, "Yea it's a good job we can all drive just in case I get too tired."

With the Jag eating up the miles on the

quiet roads they were soon past Birmingham, heading for Derby. Both boys were sound asleep and Gwen nodding off when Adrian posed the question, "Ok, Billy boy, now you've managed to kidnap all three of us it's time to spill the beans, like where the hell are you taking us, mate."

Billy answered, "Oh didn't I tell you, sorry pal, we're heading for Sheffield, well almost Sheffield anyway."

Gwen suddenly became fully awake and shouted, "Billy, what the heck are we going to a place like Sheffield for?"

"Quite simple Gwen, I've bought the Sheffield Trucker's Roadhouse and it needs a massive renovation. New kitchens, new bathrooms, more paint than you can ever imagine, new curtains and new floor coverings. Old Fred is delighted and can't wait until tomorrow morning to get his hands on the place."

"Ok Billy, got all that but where do we come into the picture. It's much too far for us to be involved, isn't it? We would spend all our days travelling back and forth and not get any work done and wear ourselves out in the process."

"Initially your comments are on line, however, please wait until we get there then you'll begin to understand the complexity of the job and like me see some solutions to help us all to come out in front." For once Billy decided to risk tea and coffee on site to save time and he led them straight upstairs via the outside exit. He opened up and welcomed them all in then explained about the living accommodation. He told them that he was going to run the weekend night shift himself He planned to spend 5 days on site with Fred and others, maybe, even Adrian and Allan by occupying two of the first floor rooms for sleeping and bathing. They next spent some time deciding what was needed on the upper floors to bring them up to scratch, they descended internally to the café. The health inspector and building inspector had just arrived so as soon as pleasantries had been exchanged they went right through the ground floor and discussed the rear porch becoming a scullery and the front annex becoming a retail shop. Billy explained what the new kitchens would look like, then mentioned the juke box and the poker machines and new style coffee machines. Billy then led them outside into the front driveway and filling station and explained, with the aid of some preliminary sketches supplied by the oil companies, what proposed changes would be made to improve traffic flow. The council experts were amazed and congratulated Billy for his ideas. They said they would expect little if any, problems with council because they were becoming more and more concerned with the state of the business both from a visual image right through to the operation side, and that aside, if they could get the business fired up again, there would almost certainly be quite a lot of extra, permanent jobs particularly for young people, which the area desperately needed.

The planning inspector asked Billy what, if any, changes would be made to staffing levels if he managed to get the place back on track. Billy said, "Gentlemen this business is running on a minimum, almost skeleton staff due mainly to the huge drop off in turnover. My projected figure should show a much improved turnover and a big increase in staff numbers. I'm certain, based on figures obtained from our

Haversby outfit that we will pull this off, and within a few months we will be scouring the countryside for good staff members. Provided you have a trade college with forward thinking staff nearby we will be training new cooks, chefs and other staff to familiarise themselves with the latest equipment and technology including the new tills and some, in fact, many, will become proficient in their trades and fill some of the gaps around the district, reduce unemployment and reduce antisocial behaviour around the city precincts. The main reason for the antisocial activities is ennui, and pure boredom. Give these people respectable, long term employment and most important of all self respect and they will lift themselves out of the morass of unemployment. I firmly believe that only they can achieve these high ideals whereas no amount of shoving or bullying will ever do it."

The council officials were dumbfounded and they stood back to think about what Billy had said realising of course, that he was quite correct. Society could not even begin to drive these listless, lazy, and unemployed people by using threats, punishments or force. Both of these two gentlemen had been in the army during wartime and knew that the same tactics didn't work out here in civilian times, and in fact in many more extreme cases, they didn't work in the army. No matter how society was thinking these days they had to create a "want to work" ethic based on making sure that there were adequate numbers of jobs out there and employers willing to train young workers, either by themselves or employing others to do so. They had to teach the youth of today how to attack each task efficiently and encourage them to want to be involved.

Billy shouted them all coffee and snacks in the café whilst they discussed all the angles. Both of the council experts were amazed at Billy's wisdom and promised that they would do all in their power to assist him to make this project work. Billy offered to take them through the upper floors to explain, what he was proposing to do but they were already satisfied and they turned to Allan and said so long as he documented each change and drew up the details and submitted them to council they would be approved and added to the current files. After well wishes and sincere handshakes all round, they departed leaving Billy and his crew ecstatic. Billy and his team began to sort out the mess on the first floor and he showed Adrian and Allan the proposed temporary living quarters, and he made the proposal that they could all travel to the new café on Thursday mornings and work through until Tuesday morning then return home for a rest. Adrian was not totally against the schedule but he thought it might be too long a week for his other lives and he suggested that he and Allan were very keen to be involved but they would travel back and forth to suit their other needs and customers. He said they would welcome the interior work whenever the weather was unfavourable but he had other jobs to finish off as well. They were particularly keen to work on the ground floor renovations and would work in with Fred and Billy to that end.

As agreed with the current owners and the estate agents, Billy and Fred set up their bedrooms and began upstairs until they were allowed to tackle the lower floor. Adrian made a start on the en suite bathrooms and walk-in wardrobes whilst Fred measured the windows and floors cleaned off walls and started painting. Alison would not be left out so she and Melissa organised shifts so one of them could babysit at home and sometimes at the café. Whenever Elizabeth was babysitting at home, Mel and Alison camped at the new café with their men folk. It was a bit messy but they soon had most of the upper floors sorted out ready for the change-over.

Billy was reluctant to close the kitchen completely and leave the lorry drivers in the lurch but there really was no other way. He had to close the kitchen completely but he had another idea quite by accident. One day he decided they needed a rest so Melissa joined him, bringing all the kids with her. [Some rest this day would be], however they camped upstairs in the refurbished rooms much to the kids delight and next morning they went off to spend the day together at the big fairground that had set up nearby. During the day Billy managed to get together with some of the food stall operators at the show ground and he was able to convince them to help themselves, and himself. He picked out the most upmarket and forward looking stall holders then offered them a proposition.

The food vans owners told him that this was their last big event for the season so they would be shutting down for maintenance and refits in preparation for the following season. Billy suggested that he could extend their season instead of them going home. He explained about the roadhouse, café refit and suggested that some of them could set up their vans in his yard and car park for 4 to possibly 8 weeks or until the café was ready to go. Billy selected the more prestigious vans and dismissed any of the lower echelons. He only needed 4 or five vans so he could be very choosy. Some of the owners jumped at the chance to extend their season and operate in one venue throughout the whole time with no time wasted on the road. The other big advantage was the much longer hours during which they could operate every day. Billy arranged for a roast dinner van, a Chinese take-away van, a fish and chip van, a tea, coffee and hot soup van, and a hamburger, hotdog and chips van, to set up near the front of the café and trade there for one month. They were encouraged to stay open 24 hrs each day if possible provided they could get staff to cooperate. One of the operators said he would canvass the non-participating stallholders with a view to annexing some of their staff members to allow them to work all through the night.

Billy was aware that the council might object to the scheme but hoped to get away with it seeing as it was only temporary and he could arrange the utilities and drainage to suit. Parking and traffic movement would not present too much trouble provided he was careful with the sighting and setup. He left it up to the traders to decide individually what hours they would operate, up to 24 hrs per day if they could get staff.

The day before change over the vans moved in and set up their stalls with Fred and Billy organising supplies of water and power and with a little help from the local plumber, who was working on the road house anyway, a temporary drainage system. Crude though this arrangement was it was far better than the original café production and better than many of the fairground facilities. Billy organised for them to use toilet facilities, showers and bathrooms, as well as laundry facilities in the roadhouse upper floors. The council did not connect with this departure from normal procedure during the first two weeks then the assistant to the health inspector turned up to sort out the problem. Apparently, some busy body or other had complained to her office about certain irregularities at the road house, so she had to enquire what was happening. Fortunately for the duration of the refit Billy was living full time on the first floor so he was available to argue the point with the health people. He was able to show her that the vans were all registered with the county council and all correctly set up, providing they had the landlord's permission to occupy the site in question, fully compliant, and considerately operated. That meant, that as long as they were operating within any of the county councils named, they had no restrictions placed on where they could, or could not, trade, providing they were not causing an obstruction to traffic. Because the vans were situated on private land

and had the landholder's permission they were free to trade for the duration of their agreement with Billy. She previously had believed that the vans were to become a permanent feature instead of using the kitchen in the café and in fact that was the message that her office had received. Billy escorted her into the café and showed her the brand-new kitchen that was almost ready to go and he showed her a copy of the agreement with the van people pointing out that they were in their second last week of tenancy. That meant that even if she had grounds to move them on they would be gone before the courts could do anything about it. The assistant health inspector could see that she was beaten and was not a happy woman. Billy said to her, "If you really think you've been wrong footed, go back to the writer of the letter and set her straight, then feel free to come back here one evening and sample the food on offer.

Amongst all the other problems, Billy had been contemplating the removal of all the extraneous fixtures and fittings. He decided that the only sensible approach was a clearing sale. He contacted a local firm of auctioneers and arranged for a clearing auction one week after he took over the ownership of the premises. They sent around some of their staff who catalogued each piece and wrote in a reserve price for the better articles which could be sold later if necessary. Quite a number of articles which Billy would have dumped, they declared were actually worth selling, even some of the floor coverings and curtains, pots and pans and assorted crockery and kitchen ware. They pointed out to him that there were many householders in the greater area around the road house who would still get plenty of use from the goods on offer. Because the carpets from the upper stories were so large, the best pieces could be cut off to fit the small terraced houses, which abounded in the vicinity.

On a bright, sunny, Saturday, the auction sale was well attended and Melissa and Billy were astounded at some of the prices people were prepared to pay for the used goods and chattels. The food vans were having a great day with buyers and spectators moving in and about as well as the travelling public moving through. The proceeds would go a fair way towards paying for the replacement furniture and kitchen appliances. Even the old gas stove brought a good price and the buyers went mad to get hold of the old fashioned slow combustion stove. Eventually some punter paid almost new price for it. The reserve prices set by the auctioneer were superfluous, everything was sold at a very acceptable price and Billy was enthralled. The food stalls feted him and his family members with free food and drink. The drink-stall lady called Billy over for a chat about her soup. She said, "Billy, a good number of lorry drivers weren't very happy with my soup because it tasted nowhere near as good as the roadhouse, café in Haversby. I believe you own and operate that venue and in fact you are the chef in charge of your kitchen and your wife Melissa is a senior cook there too, so I just wondered if you could help me out, or is it a trade secret."

"All that is true enough Nancy and there are one or two little tricks to improve the flavour provided your own taste buds are up to the challenge. I'll help you as much as I can because you are not competing with me in Haversby although, to a certain extent you may be around here, but not directly. If you promise not to set up a stall within 5 miles of my new café we can confer. Do you agree to these conditions?"

"Oh yes Billy I would never try to compete with you, ever, so please can you help me."

"Ok you need to have a good rapport with your butcher. I visit my chappie first thing every morning because he puts aside the best, meatiest bones as he breaks down the carcasses. He puts the marrow bones through the band saw to release all the goodies inside. He especially puts aside any bacon and ham bones, and again he cuts them small enough to fit my pans. As soon as I get them home I pop them in a very hot pan with a decent amount of beef dripping if I have any on hand but sometimes I have to use mutton fat or bacon fat. Stay with the pan and turn the bones over and over until every surface is seared and sealed then turn them out into the stock pot and begin adding the onions celery etc. We have a couple of stock pots made especially for the high flame heat because they have very thick, heavy bases. If I use those pots I leave the bones and stock in them and cook the soup in there. Most importantly, and this is where your own taste buds come into the picture, just before the cooking is complete, and not before, add a good slosh of Worcester sauce. I can't be any more precise than that because the quantity depends on so many variables, like pan size, weight of bone, type of bones, other vegetables like onions, leeks etc. Only you and your taste buds will know when it's correct and don't be mean with your herbs such as parsley, mint, oregano dill and chives, both plain and garlic chives when you can get them. The rest is up to you, taste, taste and taste. Add small quantities at first until you get the feel for it then you can get a bit bolder but always remember you can add more flavour and seasoning but you cannot remove it. I often experiment with spices and curries but it takes a lot of practice to get them right so I would advise you to stay away from that line of thinking."

Nancy was quite amazed at Billy's description of soup making and she replied,

"Goodness me, Billy, no wonder your lorry

driver friends didn't enjoy my soup. I just thought that you could chuck in a few vegetables and a bone or two and boil it all up until the vegetables were soft and stick it through a strainer. You know Billy I have been serving that mush up around the showgrounds for a number of years and nobody ever complained or threw it back at me, they must have all been pissed or something. I just can't wait to get started and give it a go. My customers will be amazed next season when we start up again, just you wait and see. I'll spend lots of time throughout the winter months experimenting and tasting and of course eating my special soups."

Finally, the sale was over and everyone pitched in to clean up the yard and driveway. The gentleman who had bought most of the dining room furniture asked Billy if he could store it on site until his premises were ready. He was shown up into the attic which had now been cleared out and told to put as much as he could in there. First thing on Monday morning the next phase of the refit began. The flooring experts moved into the dining area and loads of furniture began the arrive. A firm of kitchenware suppliers arrived and began sorting out the cutlery and crockery, somehow or other blending in with all the other workers. Then Roystons amusement caterers turned up with the latest and best Jukebox and before very long there was music bouncing off the walls and camouflaging all the other noise, whilst the crew from Roystons set up and installed four poker machines. Billy had to lock out the poker machines until all the other work was complete. Once the new kitchen was complete Billy began practicing with all the cooking devices. He said to Fred, who was helping with the taste tests, "This cooker is essentially the same as the one at Haversby and yet they perform differently. I'm having to familiarise myself with all the slightest adjustments to get the correct results. None of the settings seem to work out like the other one and I need to be able to synchronise the operations, and controls, just in case, and I'm sure it will happen, we have to move our staff around to cater for sickness and leave etc. If I am having these sorts of difficulties imagine how the others will cope. Fred answered with a mouth full of chocolate muffin, "You know Billy, you're just far too fussy, these muffins are right up my street. I love them. They're smashing, almost as good as Granny Elizabeth's in fact."

"Yea mate I know that but can I make them any better, even better than Granny Elizabeth's, that's the main worry."

There was only another week left before the food vans pulled out and the staff had to make everything work. The automatic fuel bowsers and the auto-tills were all working well after a couple of dodgy starts. The fuel company experts were about to depart having satisfied themselves, and Billy, that all the new equipment was up to scratch and working well, and Billy's staff competent to operate them, and maintain accuracy. The local fuel depots were organised to keep up the supply of fuel and other products such as engine oils and other fluids. All the new signage had been installed and there were already good signs that the trade was picking up almost daily. The advertisements in HEADLIGHT were having an effect on the lorry drivers especially at night, and they were making the most of the temporary food supplies until the kitchen was up to speed. Billy was still sorting out the staff members ready to fire up the kitchen the next weekend. A small number of the existing workers were keen to give the new system a fair go, so Billy was putting them through their paces to find out if they would make the grade, and one or two had already been selected and rostered ready for Saturday.

Chapter Ten

This was to be the big celebration and the advertisements had been organised, stocks of non-perishables ordered and perishables would be delivered early Friday morning. Much of the perishable foods stocks were being delivered from Phillips market garden, along with initial supplies of meats and bones from Michael's butcher shop in Haversby as well as bread and bakery products from Peter's bake house. Elizabeth and Alison with some help from Melissa had been baking like crazy ready for the big day. Haversby outlets were going to have to fill in the gaps until local suppliers were able to cope with the quantities and taste sensations required by Billy and Melissa.

By late on Friday evening all appeared to be ready for the big day. The soup pots were all bubbling away, curries and stews at the ready waiting only for the final touches Billy's 'girls' were setting out early with vans full of goodies. Michael, Peter, and Ernie, along with Phillip, and Jeffrey were all coming to Sheffield to attend the grand celebration and opening of the refurbished roadhouse, with their vehicles loaded to the hilt with essential supplies. Even Vanessa was getting into the act. She had organised her back-up staff to take over her end of the work so that she could leave mid-morning to attend the party. Everyone was up and about very early on Saturday morning ready for the storm of people who would hopefully turn up. If similar shindigs in Haversby were anything to go by this day would be another turmoil, so the sooner they got started the better it would be. In fact many lorry drivers were already calling in over night and early morning to save messing up their schedules.

Billy especially wanted to get the kitchen fired up and into top gear before the mobs from Haversby rolled in and so he did, driving everyone mercilessly to achieve results. He had agreed, in fact almost begged, the food vans to stay until Sunday night to act as back up to his kitchen and they were delighted to be part of the weekend. Lorry drivers and motoring public turned up early, were served and sent on their way as more and more lorries arrived. They were glad to see the Haversby mob start to roll in to top up the cupboards, pantry and kitchen. They had also brought along heaps of cut flowers, as well as potted plants and flowering pots, but best of all, Phillip had brought his two best flower girls who pitched in immediately, and began arranging flowers, many of which were for retail sale, as well as many for decorating the dining room. Closely behind the flower people, Billy spotted their old flower van. Not more flowers he thought but oh no, the two mushroom girls climbed down from the cab and began unloading their additions to the circus. They had brought a large amount, of fresh mushrooms for the kitchen and many more all packaged up for retail sale. In the front section of the van there were loads of dried mushrooms all packaged up ready for retail sales, as well as some for the kitchen. Billy just stood back totally dumb-founded until Phillips strident voice penetrated his thick skull exhorting him to get his hands out of his bloody pockets and give the staff a hand to unload the vans. He had planned for a very busy day before hand but now this lot amounted to a sort of bedlam and there was lots more to come, meat, bones, bread, cakes, pastries, you name it, it was all coming and soon.

Fortunately, as mentioned earlier the people who had bought the dining room furniture needed storage until they could house it in their new premises They had put the hard word on Billy to let them store it all upstairs in the attic rooms for a week or two. Billy had agreed without realising the significance of the deal. It was old Fred who caught on and he reminded Billy that it was all up in the bedrooms and attics and they had enough 'lads' to get it down and set it out in a corner of the car park for the benefit of all the crowd, who were arriving in droves. As fast as they could get the tables and chairs down a set up people occupied them, to enjoy their dinner. Billy was starting to wish there were 10 of him by late morning then he received a nice shock. He placed a large dish of curry on to the servery and turned away to get more, when a baby girl was pushed into his arms as Maude said, "This crazy bloke is your uncle Billy, Elizabeth. I hope you don't turn out as mad as he is. Hello Billy, lovely to see you again, give us a kiss. As you must have guessed this is your lovely niece 'Elizabeth, Jean'. I see you're in a king-sized mess as usual. Give Baby to Richard here whilst I get my coat off then you can show me where to make a start."

"Goodness me Maude we need you everywhere, so, can you help out with the flowers and plants, whilst I get the rest of this cooking out of the kitchen and keep these girls busy. It's not even midday yet and I am absolutely buggered. With Maude's able assistance, they began to see a little daylight and during a bit of a lull Billy looked around at the seething mob. That was when he had another severe shock, but not a pleasant one this time. He turned to Maude asking her, "Did you bring my old man with you Maude? Surely you wouldn't do that to me would you, today of all days?"

"Don't be silly Billy of course I wouldn't do that to you, not at any time without at least telephoning you first. Me and Dad are speaking to one another but only just and we wouldn't want his company and his stinking pipe on a drive like this. At least you are only half the distance away now you are here and living back in good old Yorkshire. Why did you ask about Dad anyway?"

"Just have a look over there, just inside the door examining some of the potted plants. Even with his back to us I can still smell his rotten old pipe, and the lady on his left looks like the woman who was with him in the chapel at your wedding."

"Oh my God Billy, you are right that's him alright. What the hell is he doing here today of all days?"

"Simple enough Maude he's come to see what mischief and trouble he can cause and there's not a thing I can do about it. He's probably here to see me make a fool of myself in front of all my guests"

Billy caught. Michael's eye, as he was chatting to Peter and Ernie, so he walked over to join them. He pointed out Joe O'Leary to them and they remembered the last time they had seen him in action. Michael asked what did Billy want to do about him and Billy said he didn't think they could or even should unless Joe decided to kick up a stink or cause any sort of trouble. They said for Billy not to worry, because now they were aware of the possible danger, they would stick close by him.

Joe kept his distance until late in the afternoon then he managed to get close to Billy. He called out to him asking, 'What the hell is all this, lad, everyone seems to think you own this set up. How the hell could that be. Thou wouldn't 'ave enough brass to buy a place like this. Billy was about to reply when Michael stepped forward and presented his business card and other credentials. Before saying, "I remember you from Haversby O'Leary and I'm here to tell you that if you make one wrong move here today I'll have you in a police cell so fast you won't know what's hit you. Your previous bad behaviour is still in abeyance and on record, so be very careful what you say and what you do."

"In answer to your question, Billy here and his wife Melissa are very wealthy people these days. Yes, they have bought and refitted the roadhouse and what a wonderful job they have made of it. It was in a terrible state when they bought it and needed a thorough overhaul They already own half of the roadhouse, restaurant at Haversby and they are half shares in a very big market garden and hot house set up that supplies much of the produce and other stock for the café as well as for retail sale. Most of the stock that you can see here today has been grown in their own gardens including all the cut flowers and flowering plants. They have also supplied all the mushrooms and other retail, sale stock, including all the produce that is on sale today. So, Joseph O'Leary behave yourself whilst you are here and keep away from Billy Riley. His sister Maude is around here somewhere and she can fill you in with most of the details, Billy has worked like a Trojan ever since he arrived in Haversby, mostly continuous 12 hour night shifts, sometimes seven days straight. I might add he has hardly slept this last four or five weeks since he gained control of this outfit to make this day a success, and I will not let you do anything that will jeopardise his efforts. I would advise you to get in your car and go home immediately. Poor Barbara was stunned at this revelation of Joe's character and she yelled at him, "Out Joe O'Leary, get outside now and you had better have some good excuses to explain your attitude to your only son. No wonder he hates your guts. Shame on you, Joe O'Leary.

"Come on then luv, let's get out of here. We're not wanted among his mob, who the hell do they think they are. We won't have long to wait before our lad goes belly up and runs out of money, then we'll see what 'appens to him and I hope he doesn't think he'll get any help from me. I'll just grab a quick word with our lass afore we go."

Maude and Richard were heading that way so Joe called out to them. Before Joe could start belittling Billy and Melissa, Maude jumped in with, "You've just been and gone and done it again, our Dad, you and your great big gob hole. Michael told me some of what you've said so it's time you buggered off out of here. Everything he told you about our Billy's financial status is true and he can get plenty of help from his bank and others. I'll tell you now

Dad, just have a look around this place and be prepared to duck. You see almost all the men in here at the moment are lorry drivers and if you even look like doing or even saying anything bad about our Billy these men will knock your block off. Each and every one of them think the world of our Billy and rightly so. Just be very careful what you say and do and get the heck out of here now. I'm sorry Barbara, Dad's always been like this and he only ever gets worse. He has never learned to switch his brain on before he opens his mouth. He can't bear to see either Billy or me get ahead and do well for ourselves, so he tries to belittle us especially our Billy, but he needs a lot more brains before he's clever enough to hurt either of us."

Joe and Barbara slunk out of the café, climbed into their car, with Barbara shouting and raving on at Joe, and headed for home. Michael and Billy got together and swapped a few details. Michael commented, "Where the hell does he get off Billy, I understood Maude to say that he had actually grown up but it didn't seem like it just now."

"Actually Michael, it's all my fault really. My

old man is as thick as three planks so every time I get one more step ahead of him he drops his bundle. He can't see how I can get ahead in leaps and bounds when he just stuffs up every time, He has always despised me all my life, instead of admiring me, and being proud to own me as his son. I feel so sorry for poor Barbara, she didn't deserve to cop any of this lot. He only came here today so that he could sling lots of shit at me but as usual he got it all wrong. Anyway that's the end of it so let's get back to enjoying ourselves and forget that rotten old sod. He can rot in hell for all I care. I wouldn't want to be in his shoes on the way home."

Melissa and Billy finally crawled up stairs and enjoyed a quick shower before crashing into their bed. They were completely exhausted and slept right through breakfast and finally reappeared about lunch time the next day. All the family, including the kids were patiently waiting for them to appear so they could bog into the feast that Elizabeth and Alison had prepared. New though they were the staff had risen to the occasion and had everything ticking over very nicely. Lorry drivers were still pouring in to sample the new arrangements and congratulate everyone on their efforts. Billy did a quick run around with his dip-sticks to check the fuel tanks before telephoning the fuel companies to arrange for a top up soon. He couldn't find Phillip and Michael anywhere, then someone told him, they had taken the vans back to Haversby for more stock. Cut flowers and potted flowers were in very short supply as were fresh mushrooms, greens and other vegetables. Michael had telephoned his assistant hoping to get him the process lots of sausages and hamburger meat along with a couple of sides of bacon and sundry other meats. Sliced ham for sandwiches was in short supply as were small steaks and lamb chops for mixed grills. Just after lunch the two vans pulled in ready to unload and restock so it was "all hands on deck" to attend to that. When Phillip finally caught up with Billy he said, "Hey mate I want a word with you. I need you to look me straight in my eyes and solemnly promise that you will never, ever do anything stupid like this, not ever again. If you ever decide to buy up or open another roadhouse you can consider our friendship at an end ok. I am absolutely buggered. It might be alright for you young fellows but I'm far too old for this sort of lark.

But putting all that aside mate, congratulations on a fantastic effort by you, yourself and all the family members who have worked beside you, well done. Here shake my hand pal. I reckon if you put this place back on the market immediately you'd get back all you've put into it and more. You would probably double your investment. You've reawakened the place and the lorry drivers will repay you a thousand times in the coming weeks and months and you'll probably build up a good solid local trade, like you did at Haversby as a bonus. The shop at the front is going great guns already and people are congratulating the staff on the quality, especially the flowers and vegetables. I had better schedule in a regular run up here every week, and maybe twice a week at that, unless you intend stocking the place locally."

"Not on your life Phil we'll take as much stock as you can supply and maybe much more, although we'll have to top up from local growers, if and when necessary." Billy replied.

Mel and the kids came out to join them after unloading the vans saying, "Phew, thank goodness that's done but now I suppose we still have to prepare and sell it all." Billy tried to envelope Mel and all his kids at once saying, "Well done you lot, now I know why we've got so many wonderful kids. You were a great help as you always are and now who wants free ice creams and cream buns, just help yourselves. Mum and I love you all, even when you're not helping."

The new roadhouse quickly settled down into a great business. Some of the old staff members were kept on and a few of the colleges jumped in at the chance to give their students lots of practical experience in the hospitality industry. Some of them were never going to make the grade but a few excelled and within a month or two they had gained a steady supply of workers. Billy settled down into the new routine. He soon got into the habit of loading the bigger vans and travelling up to Sheffield during the day on Thursdays and he worked through the weekend putting in 5 night shifts before returning home on Monday. He and Phillip had hunted around for a new van to replace the aging Austin. They stipulated that this time it had to be a diesel. They finally decided to buy a Toyota diesel bus. The bus had three seats mounted backwards against the front seats, with another row of three seats facing them. Billy arranged a body builder to the hinge the front legs on the forward facing seats and install heavy duty clamps to hold down the rear legs. It was designed so that the clamps could be released and the seat tilted forward to rest on the rear facing seats. This allowed for plenty of room for his family when in seating position but also lots more cargo space in the rear end. The van had a big sliding door behind the passenger seats and a full size lift up rear door. The body builder also designed and manufactured suitable shelving throughout the rear load space. Not every week but quite often Mel would load the van with any shortages and specials on Friday afternoons, then load the kids on board and drive to Sheffield to spend time with Billy. Quite often the older kids like Mathew had other agendas so they stayed home with Fred and Alison.

The new routine worked well for a few months until one Monday when Billy arrived home he found Mel bawling her eyes out in her kitchen. Billy was soon able to get to the bottom of the drama. Mel told him that Granny Elizabeth who was approaching her ninetieth birthday had collapsed with a severe bout of influenza. Unfortunately it spread onto her chest and lungs and became a serious bout of bronchitis and then into pneumonia. Her lungs were full of mucus and other fluids until she was battling to breath. The family doctor tried to get her to go into hospital or at least have an oxygen mask at home but Elizabeth was having none of that malarkey. She insisted in staying in her own bed. Billy organised for a full time nurse to attend to her needs but it was plain to see that she was slipping away quite quickly. Billy organised for Malcolm to manage the Sheffield café so he could stay home. In less than a week it was obvious that Granny would not last much longer so after school one day he took all the kids to see her having explained how things were and asking them to each see Granny, hold her hands and love her and cuddle her. Near their bedtime he asked them all to hold hands around Granny's bed and sing some of her favourite songs and hymns like "abide with me "and "Amazing Grace". He asked them to join him in a rendition of The Lord's Prayer, before going to bed. He and Mel sat beside Granny Elizabeth until she slipped into a deep sleep, never to reawaken again. Once the evening chores were completed Alison and Fred joined them for an all night vigil at her bedside. She always maintained that she had enjoyed a wonderful, happy life, especially the last few years, loving the kids and helping Billy and Melissa out in the café.

Next morning Mel and Billy cuddled their kids and told them that their Granny had gone to heaven, that she had slipped away during the night. Then they took them in one at a time to say their final farewell then the whole family moved into the room and sang "Amazing Grace" again before reciting The Lord's Prayer together.

There was a grave site located alongside her long-departed husband and three days later she was interred therein to rest through eternity. The funeral was the biggest in living memory. Mourners came from everywhere and even many of the lorry drivers attended to see her off. They held a massive wake at the roadhouse and there were flowers everywhere. Granny Elizabeth had led a reasonably quiet life but she sure got a lively funeral and she would be missed dreadfully by all who knew her. Mel and Billy's kids were devastated as were Alison and Fred. Her legend would live on forever through her cakes and pastries. Melissa and Alison had carefully saved all her recipes and instructions as well as special tips. Melissa thought that her Granny ought to have written a cookery book. Billy suggested that it was not too late to do that. He suggested that Melissa get together with Alison and write the book posthumously, which they vowed to do, with maybe a little input from Billy.

Chapter Eleven

The following day Billy had to travel back to Sheffield to give Malcolm a break. All was well up there and Malcolm had done a great job of running the outfit, which was still increasing in trade almost daily, both with passing traffic and from locals dropping in for a feed and fuel, as well as shopping for the fresh goodies in the retail store. The poker machines continued to turn over a big cash flow and the juke box was seldom silent. Fuel sales went through the roof especially dieseline for the lorries. For the most part fuel and food sales went hand in hand and they encouraged the shop sales into the bargain. The green houses at Haversby were working to their maximum due to the, out of season, potted flowers. The fields were constantly being refocussed to cope with the cut flower trade in both roadhouses and Phil was looking around for more greenhouses. New ones were expensive but the profits were good provided they were managed with skill and dexterity, and therefore a possibility in the future.

Maude and Richard made a bit of a habit of turning up at the Sheffield café and Maude always pitched in to help, especially with the bookwork which she was very competent with. Her expertise with mathematics was like gold in the bank. She could spot any errors a mile away. Billy did have contacts with a qualified accountant friend over the years and was amazed at his expertise. This chap could, and did, just run a biro or pencil down a column of figures and write the total as soon as he registered the final figure. Whilst Maude was not that clever she wasn't far behind him.

The demise of Granny Elizabeth whilst causing great sadness also left a huge hole in the roadhouse staffing arrangements. Poor old Alison, who, let's face it was now getting ready to throw in the towel and retire, which was only to be expected, had managed to keep pace with the demands of the cafe. As

Granny Elizabeth slowed down over the years, Alison shouldered the shortage and battled on coping with all the cakes and patisserie preparations, cooking and presentation always with lots of backup from Mel and Billy. Any of the roadhouse staff who showed an inclination for the cakes and pastry making were shunted along to the farmhouse to fill in the gaps in production. Alison had never taken a holiday and only took a day or two off when Billy was available to take over. Billy and Melissa had been searching high and low for experienced people the assist and eventually take control of that essential side of the business. One day just by a fluke, a coincidence in fact, He walked into the main kitchen area at the café and caught out one of his staff working on something unusual and unexpected. The young girl of about 16 years old was messing about with a small pile of pastry instead of cooking for customers. There was a tray of freshly cooked croissants fresh from the oven nearby and Billy surprised her by moving in close and asking, "Ok Belinda, what the heck are you up to."

Belinda nearly jumped out of her skin,

blushed bright red, and burst into tears, whilst muttering apologies for her activity. Billy soon settled her down ready for a talk with her about her work. Belinda told him that her mother had been a qualified and gifted pastry cook in a shop in Bristol city until her fingers became useless due to arthritis, forcing her to resign and try, unsuccessfully, to get a pension, to support herself and her only daughter. As a result they had moved to Haversby to get cheaper accommodation. Belinda had left school one year early, before taking her GCE exams. This job was their only source of income and as a sixteen year old the starting wage was minimal hence her need to work as much overtime and weekend work as possible.

Billy thought, if only her mum had explained their dire circumstances he would have been able to help. Belinda could have worked every weekend and still gone the school. He quizzed her about her ambitions concerning pastry cooking and she told him that that was her ambition and the roadhouse was only a stop gap to keep them afloat. He asked her about her Mum's hands, about how bad they were and could she still manage some tasks in the kitchen. Belinda told him that, yes her Mum could still be useful in the kitchen but could not take a full time job as a pastry cook because she could not manage many of the finer points. Billy then said, "These croissants look fabulous, is it ok if I try one. You must have done this before."

Belinda replied, "They are your croissants because I made them with your ingredients and in your time, so please have a taste."

Billy broke the end off one of the pastries and was delighted. He reckoned that that was the tastiest he had ever eaten and proceeded to scoff the whole thing. Turning round to Edith, his on duty cook, he broke another croissant in half and gave her half of it and Belinda the other half. They were delightful and Edith asked her if they always turned out like these ones. Belinda told them that they could not afford the ingredients but when she did make them they had always turned out good, with her Mum's guidance of course. However, this was her first attempt on her own without her mum to watch over her."

Edith asked her if she ever baked any other delights or was this, her sole attempt at fame. What else do you cook at home."

Belinda replied , "I can and do bake, and present all or any of the cakes like those that we sell here in the café and shop whenever we can manage to pay for the ingredients."

"Ok, that's it then. Edith get on the phone and see if any of our reserves are available to help you until midnight. I'll take wonder woman here to meet Alison, provided you can manage here, that is." Billy said.

"Yes boss can do. I'll call Robert or Andrew. We'll be fine."

Billy drove Belinda out to the farm and introduced her to Alison. The two ladies hit it off together right from the start and with Alison's guidance they fired up the big gas oven and the AGA stove to begin cooking up a storm. Next morning he arranged to meet Belinda at her home hoping to meet her mother, Thelma, because he'd just had a great idea. The next morning he arrived at the very humble, old cottage where Belinda and Thelma were living. They were both quite embarrassed to have visitors in their humble home but Billy soon put them at ease. He told them about the arrangements he had with the social welfare people and offered to sort out their problems. He arranged to collect Thelma and drive her to see the welfare people where a doctor would be able to assess her level of disability and work out how much assistance they could offer her. He took them to meet Melissa who handled all the negotiations with the department. Mel told them, that once Thelma had been assessed and classified she could work out a suitable salary level and working hours, where she could work beside Belinda and coach her and train her to be a pastry cook. With the two of them working together alongside Alison the supply of cakes and pastries was once more assured. Belinda would be upgraded according to her abilities and usefulness not relying on her age grouping. Billy was quite worried about the quality of their accommodation and was planning to fix that. The elderly gardener who had lived in the old cottage near the farmhouse for many years had succumbed to the latest flu epidemic and passed away, thus leaving the cottage empty.

Billy caught up with his father-in-law Fred and his builder mate Adrian, arranging for them to refurbish the cottage, adding all mod-cons such as bathroom, kitchen, laundry, and toilet as well as central heating, which could be run off the nearby boiler, which supplied the greenhouses. Once the cottage was finished he offered it to Thelma and Belinda. During the upgrade they were mindful of Thelma's disability and were able to claim more funds from the welfare to put in special taps and door handles and generally bring the place up to invalid status. Having the girls close by made so much sense and they were delighted with the cottage. The new taps made life so much easier as did the door handles. With some of their own furniture and fittings and the best of Harold's furniture they were well set up and very happy. They only had a short walk from their cottage to the farmhouse nearby ready to start work. There were lots of hot baths and showers available. After a hard day kneading, rolling, pounding, and cooking, this was such a great relief and even Thelma's hands were improving although they would never fully recover. She could at least help with much of the rough work, even though she couldn't use the icing and finishing tools. However, Belinda had plenty of patience and artistic talents to make a superb job of finishing off. Once again they were able to supply both cafes with first class muffins, pasties and cakes. Alison still found plenty of spare time to help out and even Mel and Billy joined in when time permitted.

Billy and to a lesser extent Mel realised that they were pushing themselves way too hard and also not spending anywhere near enough time with their family so they had a round table conference, as the saying goes, to try to resolved the problem before it became too serious. It was Malcolm who inadvertently solved the conundrum. He had been going out with a very lovely girl, one of the staff members as it turned out, who, apart from being a lovely looking girl, was a hard and competent worker in the roadhouse kitchen. This lovely couple were actually hoping to get married quite soon but like Billy and Melissa before them were having great difficulty finding some suitable accommodation. The only cottages near the roadhouse and in the whole town were decrepit old hovels. Billy called the two of them out to the farm one evening because he had managed to work out a possible solution. When they were all enjoying coffee and cakes Billy suggested, "I reckon you are both looking too close to home and need to broaden your horizons."

Malcolm replied, "That may yet have to be, Boss but we don't want to spend all our time running backwards and forwards."

Billy said, "He could only concur with that theory so maybe a change of workplace might solve the problem."

Malcolm retorted strongly, "Are you thinking of giving us both the sack and wanting to kick us out of the café and leave us without jobs after all the years that we've toiled on your behalf? Surely you haven't forgotten how I helped you out when Granny Elizabeth passed away, and after all, who was best man for you when no one else was available?"

"Whoa Malcolm you're getting a bit ahead of yourself here. It is as a result of the funeral efforts that I realised there was a great solution to all of our problems right under our noses, that is if you two want it, and are ready to get married."

"The only reason we are still unwed is because we have nowhere to live. Neither of us wants to live with parents and in-laws."

"Ok, how's this for a solution to your problems and mine. There is enough accommodation at the Sheffield roadhouse that will take the two of you a life time to fill with kids. If you Malcolm are ready to take over and manage the Sheffield café and this lovely girl of yours is willing to back you up the opportunity is yours. As you know it is fully furnished and complete with linen and utensils ready to move in. You only need your personal clobber and it is yours. We will always be beside you and ready to help out as necessary but the job is yours if you think you can step up into my shoes. There will be a substantial increase in salary for both of you, so have a think about that and let us know as soon as possible. Thank you both for giving us your time to night, and no I will not be paying you overtime for tonight." Malcolm jumped up, grabbed Rosalind, his girl, pulled her into a huge hug and delivered lots of juicy kisses to her lips before turning to Billy, grabbing his hand and shaking it as though he was trying to break it off before saying, "Yes Boss of course we will take it on gladly. We were hoping that something like his might come our way but not here with you and Melissa. Melissa and Rosalind were cuddling one another and laughing joyously with plenty of tears to boot. Well what a night a whole heap of problems solved without any pain.

"So you two do you have a suitable time schedule to get yourselves sorted or will you move in tonight? When and where is your wedding likely to be? You've been thinking about this day for a long time obviously so tell us, WHEN will it be?"

"This is not the first time that you've backed me into a corner, but there will be no instant decision, this time. We had better get out of your hair now Boss, and Boss Lady because we have people to see and things to organise. Do you have a change over date set for Sheffield roadhouse as yet?"

"Hardly, you pair have just sprung this on us tonight; but as soon as you can arrange it. Go home now and talk it over with your parents, make some careful decisions between you all then get married as soon as possible. If you need any help just yell out. If it suits you Malcolm, you can start at Sheffield before you get married. You and I can go through the books and procedures such as when and where to reorder stock, how to run the petrol pumps, dip the tanks and a million and one other things as well. If I rearrange the rosters starting on Monday, you and I can camp up at Sheffield and get you started. You will need a suitable vehicle to get around town and come home on your days off so you can drive up in my old Austin Omnivan. I have just had it fully serviced and it is ready to roll so here are a set of keys, you two are fully mobile now. I am assuming that Rosalind has a drivers licence if not we can soon organise one for her Young Alexandra Forrester should be able to step up and fill your shoes here with Melissa's help. He is a senior cook now so will benefit from the experience and maybe lift himself up to be a chef one day soon. Always remember, we are all going to be behind you, and in that, I include

Phillip, Michael and Peter. We all need you to succeed to protect our investments in the project so good luck both of you.

"What can we say, Boss, thanks, thanks and thanks again, Rosalind does have her licence to drive, and let me say this, I promise that you will never regret what you are doing for us. We have seen what happened to yourself and Melissa once given a chance and we can and will emanate your examples, thanks again and goodnight." Malcolm Concluded as he stood up ready to leave.

Early the following morning Billy caught up with Alexandra at the café and pulled him aside for a chat over coffee and cakes in a corner of the restaurant where they would not be disturbed or over heard. Billy explained the situation to Alex then went on to offer him the top job besides himself and Melissa. Billy explained what would be expected of him, over and above the duties he already carried out, and quite importantly, the extra salary that went with the job. He asked Alex if he believed that he could manage the job and keep control of staff and all the inevitable paper work that the job created. Alex said in reply, "Thank you Boss for believing in me and giving me this great opportunity to improve my position within the firm. I was a bit concerned about where the job was leading me and wondering what the next steps would entail. I never dreamed that Malcolm would move on and leave a vacancy here for me. As you probably are aware I am currently walking out with Pamela Jameson and I don't have a clue where that is going to take me, us, in fact, but having an opportunity like this puts me in a stronger position. Her Mum is quite a sweetie and quite a bit soft on me, but her Dad is a bit of a tyrant. He expects Pamela to eventually marry a millionaire or someone from the aristocracy .Pamela is still only sixteen and I am almost eighteen so we are looking a long way ahead but if I can show her Dad that I have good prospects for our future he might ease up on me. Hey Boss I've just had a thought, now that Pamela is sixteen and in her last year of high school could she get a part-time job here at the café, maybe weekends, say? She has been working seasonally at the market garden since she was twelve."

"Ok then Alex you can begin by working alongside Malcolm for the rest of this week then you will have to work with Melissa because I have to go with Malcolm to Sheffield to show him the ropes. Ask Pamela to come and see me so I can assess her ability and work out a suitable roster that won't interfere with her school work schedules. This final year is very important and she would not want to miss out on her GCE. If she's studying domestic science we may be able to help her along the way. I would want to see her mother as well, so see what you can arrange. You and Pamela will not be working together, I would require her to work with me in here and Melissa will teach her some basic book keeping and accountancy if she is good at arithmetic. Also if Pamela is interested in pastry cooking she can be rostered on to assist Thelma and Belinda in the farmhouse kitchen. I expect to spend a few weeks up at Sheffield with Malcolm then I will return and take over here. As I'm sure you will be aware Melissa is in charge of all the bookwork and paperwork around here so get up close with her and get to know what she requires of you in that line to minimise her workload. If you can present all the invoices and dockets in an orderly file Melissa will take it from there. Are there any things you need to ask about now before you get started."

"Oh gosh, Boss I'm totally overwhelmed by all this. This is something that I have dreamt of since I started here and it will take a day or two to sink in. Thank you so much for giving me this opportunity and I won't let you down, I promise. Also I'll have a chat with Pamela and her mum because I'm sure she will benefit particularly working with Melissa and Thelma, which is much better than gardening."

"Well Alex, that's great, and remember; when you do get around the father-in-law, let us know and we will shout you a wedding breakfast to remember. That should impress him since it's usually the brides family's prerogative to attend to all that."

Later when Billy and Melissa caught up with each other over lunch Melissa endorsed all that Billy had arranged because, she needed help with the books and Thelma needed a spare hand or two with the pastry business, especially at the weekends. Billy marvelled at the way so many factors of the business were all coming together.

Meanwhile Phillip and his loyal band of workers were really going great guns. The disabled group were quite amazing and a great inspiration to all the able bodied people in the group and it was becoming increasingly obvious that their participation was a very valuable resource. One or two of them had found a comfortable niche in the roadhouse with even some mentally imperfect people doing very well in the tasks that was within their scope and ability. Because there was such a huge diversity of occupations available in the gardens and roadhouse combined, most handy-capped people could find a suitable niche to suit their abilities. As you would realise Billy and Phillip both encountered a number of obstacles, some of which were insurmountable, but that was only to be expected.

Malcolm and his wife, Rosalind were well accepted in Sheffield and the business continued to flourish. Often one or more lorry drivers took time out to drop a line into the "Headlight" editor raving on about their experiences at both of the roadhouses. This type of advertising is far superior to businesses pushing their own barrows which Billy was prone to do from time to time.

Phillip had accidentally made contact with the editor of "Home and Gardens" magazine after a chance meeting when she had visited the roadhouse for a meal whilst on her travels northwards to amass material for her magazine. She was currently in a state of shock whilst examining the display of cut flowers and flowering plants in the roadhouse shop, many of which were well out of season. The shop assistant steered her into the café where Phil was enjoying a nice curry for his lunch. The lady introduced herself and her occupation and presented Phil with her business card. Phil, of course was amazed as he got to his feet and invited the lady, Margret Jameson, to take a seat at his table and offered to provide her with a meal of her choice and drinks to wash it down. Margaret took in a deep breath and declared that Phil's curry smelled so good so could she please have one of those and a pot of coffee.

Whilst the waitress was attending to her meal, Phil put his credentials on the table, so to speak, and telling Margaret a little of the history of the roadhouse to date. He had slipped a note to the waitress for Billy to attend if he was somewhere nearby. It turned out that Billy was helping and instructing in the kitchen at that time, so he came out to meet their visitor. Phil got to his feet as Billy approached saying, "Margaret, This is Billy who I mentioned, and Billy, this lady is Margaret Jameson who is editor of your favourite magazine, "Home and Gardens."

Billy was stunned and delighted to meet his favourite editor. He organised the waitress to bring him coffee and settled down for a chat with this prestigious lady, who he hoped could stay for a while and have a good look around. Margaret said she would love to spend the rest of the day with Phil and Billy because there appeared to be more of a story here than at her previous proposed destination. Margaret asked if there was somewhere suitable for an overnight stay and could she use their telephone to re-address her itinerary.

Billy said, "My wife and I always have a couple

of rooms available for passing waifs strays like yourself, and you can use one of the phones in my office. I'll just grab another coffee then we can get going as soon as you are ready."

Margaret replied, "Oh I didn't expect to barge into your lives, but if that suits you and your wife, I would love to take advantage of your generous offer."

Billy quickly called Melissa on one of the other phones and invited her to join in for the tour of inspection, which she gladly accepted and promptly appeared at the café dressed in jeans and work boots. Margaret returned to the table to announce that all was well with her domain and she was free for the rest of the day. Phillip led the way out to the cars and drove them all around to the farmyard where they inspected the packing areas before tackling the mushroom growing sheds where Margaret was thrilled to see mushrooms growing. She said "I wasn't aware that anyone could grow mushrooms like this in sheds and I only believed that there was one variety of edible mushrooms and all the others are poisonous." She was enthralled at the drying plant and realised immediately it's potential. Her fountain pen was scribbling frantically, trying to record all the information. Suddenly she stopped writing and turned to the crew to ask if it was ok to publish all this information. Billy grinned and replied, "We had to start from scratch with very little previous knowledge and little or no ongoing assistance. This lot was all trial and error and plenty of the latter, however we persevered until we believe we now have the correct formula. This all looks like a walk in the park now but there are many secrets that we will not divulge to anyone, especially someone like yourself. We have to protect ourselves from plagiarism. Phil particularly has worked very hard with some of his staff to get to this excellent scenario. There were plenty of disasters along the way and plenty of heartaches to the point that, on many occasions, we were close to aborting the whole scheme. Patience and perseverance won out in the long run so we are not likely to divulge any critical information to yourself or any other party.

"Ok, guys, I would not want to know all the how's and wherefores and would not divulge any secret information deliberately. I will submit copies of my writing to each of you before publication, so you can check and edit all the ins and outs, before going to print, and that also applies to any of these photographs as well".

Billy said, "Ok Phil, lead on, where to next?"

"I thought we might stroll around the flower fields next because it looks like we might get a shower. We can look around the hot house later, no matter what the weather."

After a good look around the growing fields, mainly the flowers but quite a lot of the seasonal vegetables Phil led them on into the first hot house and explained an outline of how it all worked, then they went inside the larger hot houses where most of the out of season flowers were growing. Some were growing in pots whilst others were planted in the ground beds because they were sold as cut flowers not potted flowers.

Margaret asked, "I understand that you can prepare bulbs, corms and root stock to grow out of season but don't you have problems getting them to flower out of season".

Billy replied, "Over to you Phil, more your department than mine, but please be careful. Editors and journalists have big ears as you know and even with all the promises, the slightest slip could set us back years, and open up the doors to our opposition."

Phil answered the question very carefully as he said, "Like the mushrooms Margaret, patience and perseverance, trial and error, with many disappointments along the way. I had to think like a flower and work out what triggers the plant to send out flowering shoots and ultimately flowers. Once I worked out how I then had to work out when. Flowering is not instantaneous. I had to time each type of flower to be sure exactly how long it would take to mature, once the stimulus had been delivered, then work out when to deliver the stimulus. In many cases the exact timing isn't important, but Xmas time, Easter, and Mothering Sunday we have to be exact. You have to be a little bit insane to run a show like this and believe me we don't always get it right. We often have to rely on Billy and the roadhouses [two of them now] to clean up our mess and mistakes. It often amazes me what, and how much, these two outfits can absorb, not only in flowers but also in vegetables. One of Billy's favourite saying is bent and miss shaped carrots taste exactly the same as straight ones. All that means is, that we have very little waste either in the flower department or in the vegetable department."

Billy then added, "So there you have it Margaret, or at least all that we are prepared to share with you and your readers. We'll retire back to the farmhouse for lots of hot showers, then back to the café for a choice meal in the restaurant for dinner. After a jolly good feed we'll return to the farmhouse and a nice comfy bed."

"Well Billy, Melissa, and Phil, words could not possibly express my thanks to you all for a wonderful afternoon. I am blown away by what I have seen here today and I hope you will invite me back again for another look at your garden."

"Margaret, it has been our pleasure to entertain you here today but there is still more to be seen at the farmhouse. We have a team of pastry cooks working in our huge kitchen baking up all sorts of pastries and cakes for sale in our two cafes, and retail shops. About a second visit to the gardens, try to come in the early spring next time when our fields will be abloom with spring bulbs like daffodils and tulips. Our fields full of spring bulbs are a real sensation and should not be missed. We will look forward to reading your comments on our enterprises, thank you for your visit, even though it was accidental"

The tour of the farmhouse and especially the kitchens truly amazed Margaret. Once again there were sincere thanks all round before this hungry crew headed off back to the restaurant for dinner where Margaret was once more amazed to find such a high class premises outside any major city and the diverse menu was as always, stunning. She commented on the menu stating, "This is truly great, both the selection and the quality of the meal. I was expecting a typical roadhouse mixed grill not a truly gourmet dining experience like this, thank you so much. I will enjoy relating my experiences to my readers and I only hope I can do justice to your business in the telling.

I have seen such a huge variety here today, much more than one story. I might just write an overview in the first instance and follow it up with separate segments on each of the sections in consecutive issues. I will probably need to separate your story into 4 or 5 segments. Billy, would you be happy for me to begin with a short segment on your journey to get here to the cafe, and how you made a comfortable niche for yourself."

Billy wasn't too happy to be made to look like some sort of hero so he replied, "Yes Margaret, but only the actual road trip and nothing prior to that day. You can begin with the story of my stowing away on a low loader to get here but not WHY it was necessary. I will not approve it any other way thank you, nor will I allow you to print any details of my injuries."

"Just a point, Margaret, we have touched on our employment of a good many handicapped personnel. Would you be happy to do one complete segment on how that works and benefit both us and the handicapped?"

"Of course Billy, I had already pencilled that aspect in for one of the five segments and I would like to include your interaction with the schools and colleges as well."

"Thank you for that Billy, and I will honour my earlier promise to you, that I will submit all my text to you for approval before going to print. Not a single word will be printed unless you are all happy with the content. I am so pleased with today's outcome that I will not do anything to jeopardise that trust. I will send you preprint copies of each issue in the first place to ascertain that we are all in harmony."

When the first preprint copies were available Phil and Billy were delighted, with the content and presentation. Margaret had taken the time out to travel to Haversby and display them personally. Everyone was looking forward to the next issues of "Home and Garden" magazine and the expected extra trade especially with the flower presentation and shop trade. Billy said to Vanessa and Melissa, "It looks like we might have to increase the size of the retail premises to cope with all this activity."

Vanessa replied, "I must whole heartedly agree with that, Billy I'll give our architect friend a buzz and see what can be done. I've already been thinking along those lines anyway even with the current trade. We need to have two more tills to cope with the volume of trade and there is nowhere to put them so we need a complete rethink.

Raphael was available the next day so he duly arrived and began sketching and measuring. He thought it would be necessary to put in new foundations, outside the existing walls, so that the shop could continue trading throughout the building phase. He said that providing council was in agreement they would increase the height of the external walls then use steel girders over the roof of the shop and put in a new ceiling before dismantling the old shop. He said there would be some inconvenience during construction but it would be kept to a minimum. Billy said they could knock up a few signs up and direct the customers to the rear door alongside the jukebox and just close the shop counter down for a day or two.

As before the council engineer put in an appearance to vet the project and as before he had very little input and quickly signed the work over to Adrian and Allan to get stuck into the job. Once the walls were constructed and approved a large crane was called in to lift the overhead beams into place and very soon the building shell was complete. Some of Phillips team of workers stepped in one weekend to re-arrange the interior and complete the project. Unfortunately they were not quite ready when the first issues appeared in the magazine and the first two weeks were shear pandemonium. The outside crew worked flat out to keep enough stock on the shelves and assist wherever they could. Also the pastry cooks went into overdrive and some of the extra café workers jumped in to help at the farmhouse. Once again, as expected, the disabled staff came up to scratch, and were happy to get many extra hours of work.

Melissa and Billy's oldest family members were keen to get involved with any section of the business that needed assistance both at home and at Sheffield. Mathew in particular was quickly becoming part of the outfit and would soon be running and managing one or more of the departments on his own. The retail shop now had become a vital part of the business providing much extra employment for their staff. The local people were patronising the shop rather than travelling further afield for their needs and thus making even more employment opportunities. As promised Margaret, the editor of "Home and Gardens' returned not only for the spring flowers but a few times in between. She was completely mesmerised by all the activity and the speed that changes were being made to further improve the operation.

Malcolm and Rosalind were doing a great job at Sheffield and they were very popular with the locals. Following Billy's example, Malcolm was always looking out for ways to improve, not only the turn over, but also the profit margin. Like Billy, Malcolm had worked together with the senior schools and colleges in the area to get some extra short term help and more especially teach and train new staff so there would always be spares around when needed. Melissa spent quite a lot of time with Rosalind to show her how to manage the paperwork and again more especially to get a commitment from the social service department to employ a few handicapped personnel around the café. Without the market garden there were limited opportunities at Sheffield but there was always lots of domestic work which no-one else relished anyway. Once Rosalind was competent with the enormous amount of paperwork, that only a few handicapped workers created, Melissa left her to it. She was quite competent at running the ordinary company books, wages schedules, and all the daily paperwork. The two of them, Malcolm and Rosalind had melded themselves into a very efficient team because they both had sufficient skills and talents to help each other as and when needed.

All went along very easily at Sheffield until about 6months later when Rosalind had a few unsettling and nauseous mornings. She quickly realised that she had missed her monthly visitor and just might be pregnant. A quick trip to the nearby Pharmacy for a pregnancy test kit proved this to be true so she followed it up with a visit to the doctor for confirmation and blood tests. She kept well enough on the whole to continue with attending to the office work which fitted in nicely as she didn't need to be there the all the time especially early mornings. Towards the end of her confinement they rallied all the grand mammas and other female members of both families to attend as necessary and Melissa kept the books up to date. By that time the colleges and their own cooking and business schools were paying big rewards with a steady flow of personnel to help run the café and fuel business. These together with the input by the handicapped people assured Malcolm of a smooth operation.

Finally the big day arrived and was set in motion with the breaking of her waters just before entering her office. She had a fairly long wait until the head began to show and the little beggar was helped out into the world. The baby turned out to be a sweet little girl and everyone was delighted. Billy's family was getting quite big by then and there was lots of help both domestically and business wise to fill in any gaps until Rosalind was ready to take over the reins again.

Chapter Twelve

By the time that Rosalind had delivered her baby, Emily, Mathew was looking forward to being more in charge of his own outfit and it came from an unsuspecting direction. The owner of the Roadhouses at Grantham and Newark had recently passed away. There had been an armed robbery at the Newark branch and the owner manager had been badly hurt and shortly afterwards passed away. His dear wife had no hope of continuing with running the businesses herself and tried, without much success to employ a manager for each of the two roadhouses and eventually someone suggested that she should contact the bloke over Haversby way who was running two roadhouses anyway and see if he could help her. Melissa, Billy, and Mathew discussed the situation over mealtimes for a week or so until finally Melissa said Billy should take a day off and pop over to Grantham and check it out.

As a result Billy went for a drive taking Mathew with him. Billy handed the keys of his latest Jaguar to Mathew and climbed into the passenger seat. Mathew just stood beside the car and said, "Wow! Gosh Dad, do you want me to drive over to Grantham."

"Only if you reckon you are up to it son. You'll find it much easier to handle than any of the other vehicles so hop in and have a go. Just be careful with the power until you get the feel of it. With all the bravado of youth, Mathew found the Jaguar a delight to drive and they were soon cruising along the highway to Grantham. The journey was about 90 miles through the cities of Coventry and Leicester so it proved to be a good experience for Mathew who coped well with the big car and was thoroughly enjoying the experience. After about two and a half hours Billy guided Mathew to the ancient roadhouse. He told him as they drove along that this and the Newark venue were the pioneers of this type of service centre at a time when most businesses closed their doors at five or maybe six o'clock five days per week. However in more recent times the whole outfit had been declining in trade and the buildings needed the same treatment as Sheffield unless the owners had finally decided to improve it since he had last visited there on their trips to Spalding. It was situated alongside the A1 highway as was the Newark café.

It was quite obvious as they parked up in the yard that the premises were in dire need of refurbishment the petrol pumps were ancient and very slow at best and some of the pumps were displaying , "Out of Order signs". Mathew was very dismayed at first sight and it only got worse inside. They had deliberately arrived unannounced so they could get a better overall feeling of the services, staff attitudes cleanliness, and general state of the business. Mathew was so badly disappointed that he would have walked out and driven straight back home but Billy was really quite pleased. If he bought the place the more run down it was the more likely-hood of squeezing down the price. He'd always considered that he would have to carry out a complete rebuild and restructure as he had done in Sheffield. Once they had looked around the place and raised a few curious eyebrows Billy asked for the owner. The lady was over in the house at the rear of the premises, so they walked over and rang the door bell.

The lady was still in her nightwear and dressing gown and very embarrassed to be caught out so. Billy apologised and explained who they were and why they were there.

He offered to go for a walk around the site to allow time for the lady to dress and gather her thoughts together. The lady said, "No of course that won't be necessary. I already have the coffee machine on the go so you can sit down and enjoy some refreshments whilst I get myself organised"

Billy replied, "Thank you so much, it has been a long drive and we certainly need coffee I was just wondering if you might be able to get your agent or better still your solicitor to attend our discussions. That would save much time at a later date and there would be fewer chances of any misinterpretation and essential legal inclusions."

"That's a good idea, William. I'll give them both a call then get dressed. Please help yourselves to coffee, I'm sure you can work out how to make this silly machine perform better than I can, and here are some cakes to go with it"

Once they were alone Mathew enquired, "What are you thinking Dad, Will you buy this place and what about the other one?"

"Well Mathew that will depend on you and you alone. If I buy it I will have to find a manager to run it and that might be a nightmare. We are talking about continuous 24 hr. operation like our other two roadhouses. Of course the whole place will need to be refurbished or rebuilt like Sheffield was including this house and the staff accommodation. We would need to first contact the fuel companies and hope to get the driveway and bowsers sorted out, new road signs and pay kiosk like Sheffield.

The other place at Newark I will not even consider except as a development site. If this place can be brought back to at least Sheffield standards the other one will only ever be a suburban petrol station. It would never pay to run two separate kitchens. It would only be a quick snack bar and I wouldn't want any part of that. If it was 80 or so miles away we might be able to encompass that but I think it would just be a lot of extra work that we don't need. If I bought that site I would offer it up for lease only, as a petrol station, and the lessee could then decide whether to operate 24 hrs or some lesser amount to suit his or her needs. In fact if I do buy it and lease it out I will limit the hours so that it won't clash with this one and we'll only need to refurbish this one to our standards."

"That might even suit me, Dad. I could run it for you and Mum, or if you both help me I would consider setting up on my own. I really believe I could make a success of it if you give me a try, I would probably miss the life in the kitchen though because like you I love that side of the business. What do you think?"

"I think you are jumping the gun a bit, mate. Mum and I were hoping you would want to take over and run this outfit as manager of the whole outfit. I am confident that you can do that, as Malcolm is doing in Sheffield. Like Malcolm, you'll have all our experience and backing behind you and I was hoping that your sister, Elizabeth will want to join you. She has worked alongside your Mum in dealing with the paperwork side of our business as well as the kitchen side of things. Elizabeth is great working with the new fuel tills and consoles. So by working together you should be able to make a go of it. You two always seem to get on well together and Mum and I will run over here regularly until you get it all sorted."

"Gosh! Dad, that would really be great and I am sure Beth and me can run it for you. Thank you Dad, I will never forget this day, I'm really stoked so let's be having a look at the figures."

The figures were not great even though this was the only decent roadhouse anywhere around and it was 24 hr at that. With heaps of great food and a new forecourt the figures will surely fly to great heights. After almost day long discussions and arguments a suitable deal was tabled. It resolved around the down grading of the premises at Newark into a normal service station not 24hrs and a suitable lessee or manager found to take it on. As it turned out the fuel companies were able to set up much of the necessary infrastructure and they each had a list of potential operators in both categories. One fuel company was keen to lift their profile in the area and were prepared to buy the site and lease it out as a 12 hour only service station with only limited take-away food and snacks using a water bath type of food warmer to provide instant meals, to be cooked in a small but renovated kitchen behind the counter. A deep fryer was to be the main appliance, along with a heavy duty toaster and electric kettle for tea and coffee. The main part of the dining area/café was in poor condition so it would be converted into a lube bay with electric hoists and tyre fitting utilities. The site was quickly sold off to that ends and the whole property upgraded to their specifications.

This simplified part of the negotiations but caused a considerable delay in the proceedings. The service station idea was inserted into the deal to take over the Grantham site as a condition of sale, binding the whole business together. Once the fuel company came on board and signed a purchase document for Newark the rest of the deal became straight forward. The fuel company moved very quickly before anyone could out bid them and duly signed up the papers.

Once the details of the Newark site were completed, Billy, Mathew and Elizabeth went for a trip to Grantham to arrange the final details. They arranged with Shell oil company managers to meet them at the site to discuss them becoming involved with the update. Billy was expecting a similar arrangement to Haversby and Sheffield, both of which had worked well, and continued to work very efficiently. The oil company was a bit reticent to repeat the previous deals due to changes in world financial affairs. They finally agreed to disagree, shook hands and departed leaving Mathew and Billy down hearted and somewhat despondent about the whole deal. Billy didn't wish to spread his wings too far and go it alone although he was quite sure the bank would be able to carry the debt in his name; with all his assets combined, it looked rosy enough. Mathew was looking quite upset at this point but all was not lost because the company said they would have a really good look over the proposals and make a decision in due course. Mathew asked, "What will you do now Dad? Can we pull out or are we stuck with the old type of pumps?"

"Steady on pal, all is not lost yet. We can do a partial change over to improve the fuel side of the business and everything else is as we discussed. I have only spoken with Shell about the update so that leaves us Mobilco, Esso, maybe Texaco, and British Petroleum as well. Although I will leave BP until last because they appear to be taking over Newark and will be hard pressed physically, as well as financially. Mobilco came along with us in Sheffield as you know, and Esso were also runners up and were very disappointed not to be included. So home we go and do more research. Even if we don't manage to pull off the full modernisation, we'll end up with a system much closer to that than we have at the present.

Mathew folded his sister, Beth, into his arms before replying. "Yea, thanks Dad we have got all that and we want you to know that we are one hundred percent behind you. We want this chance and will give it all our very best. When can we get started on the kitchens and the rest of it."

The contract gives us possession at the end of the month so we need to be organised by the first day of the next month. Our architect, Raphael will travel over here starting on Monday to make preliminary sketches and get things rolling."

Once back home and everything checked out Billy, and Mathew shut themselves in the office to begin negotiations with fuel companies. It was probably going to take a long time to work out a plan similar to the existing outfits. The world financial situation was a bit of a worry and the timing of the restoration was certainly bothering. Billy and Mathew went full steam ahead to restore the premises and if the fuel company didn't keep up that was no problem. Given time, one or more of them would have surplus funds which they needed to disperse sensibly. The main problem for Billy was that he had to allow for the future installation of wiring and pipe work so that nothing was duplicated. There is nothing worse than renovating a property then having to dig it all up later to install the necessary infrastructure.

At this juncture Adrian and Allan were called in

for a conference to decide whether they wanted a part of the operation or was it a port too far for them. Similarly Old Fred was approached and his first reaction was, "Hell you guys, didn't I make it clear enough at Sheffield, no bloody more, I'm too old for all this. When are we going over there for a look and measure up? At least it's a bit closer this time. Is there somewhere Alison and I can camp up whilst we get stuck in."

Billy said. The owner is ready to move out as soon as we can set up some sort of management team to take over. We'd only need to set up a time and date to run a stock take and help her to pack and move out. Like Sheffield there's quite a lot of camping space that certainly needs upgrading but will do for now, once we eliminate all the vermin. The kids are all eager to get over there especially at weekends the whole mob of them will inundate the place. Beth is very keen to sort out all the bookwork and assist in the kitchen. As far as the main building was concerned Billy assured Adrian, Allan and Fred that they would not in any way be involved with any of that. A whole new two storey building was planned and would be contracted out to one of the big building firms. Time was going to be the essence of the contract so a large firm with all the equipment and where-with-all was needed to expedite the construction. He needed to reopen the catering side as quickly as possible so a big firm like Whimpy would be invited to tender. At this point in time Billy asked Mathew to ring up Esso in the first instant then Texaco who both having missed out with both of the two previous sites just might get excited and join in this time provided they could raise the finance. He reckoned this would be a good try out for Mathew, and Beth came in and sat beside him to assist with any negotiations. Beth had looked up the files and had both the previous contracts in her hand. The Esso executives were quite keen to get on board and promised to give the proposal a fair hearing but pointed out that it was not a decision to be made lightly and would have to go before the next board meeting. When pressed by Matt they promised to convene an emergency board meeting with a view to get an early resolution.

Billy was very impressed because the two youngsters had put up a very solid case.

"So where to next Dad do we ring Texaco now whilst we are in the mood." Asked Matt.

"Yes please, Matt the two of you can do this deal without me sticking my nose anywhere near it, good luck."

Texaco were very receptive to the deal because they had lost the last one, by a narrow margin, even after organising suitable finance. However, it also meant that most of the deal was done before they started this time. The money had been put aside in a special account and left there to gain interest over the intervening time. No other serious program had been presented in the meantime so they were ready to talk 'turkey'. Two senior executives arranged to be on site [Grantham] at 10 o'clock the following morning so Matt and Beth called up their solicitors and they all went over there with the legal advisors and Billy who was needed to sign all the papers if he was in agreement.

The talks next day went very well because Texaco really wanted a big, 24hrs site on a main road. The huge sealed yard around the buildings meant there was ample room for even the largest of lorries to manoeuvre around and with 4 diesel pumps or bowsers as the Americans called them they would be well set. The company was dead against operating on a dual site and demanded exclusive access. Mathew stuck to his guns and pointed out that most of the lorries were contracted to the fuel companies and had no choice but if the site was exclusive it would not be available to many of the trucking firms. This would leave a shortage of café, as well as fuel customers. Beth said that her research was showing that most of the fuel companies, theirs included, had duel access to the credit cards for example BP and Shell Mex also accepted Esso cards.

Eventually the company reluctantly accepted the deal and there were handshakes all round. The deal was so comprehensive that Billy would not need to spend a penny on the exterior or the yard and they would end up with the very latest equipment direct from America.

Whilst the kids were sorting out the fuel business, William had arranged to meet his architect friend on site. Raphael pointed out all the problems associated trying to upgrade the existing buildings and bring them up to the standards that he and Melissa demanded. He said they would end up with a hotchpotch arrangement that would not be at all satisfactory. Billy needed to keep trading during any alterations so Raphael suggested that he could keep the kitchen and fuel business open serving take-away meals only with a slight change in the menus and recipes. That meant they could close off the dining area and demolish it giving them sufficient room to build around the old buildings which would then be demolished once the new set up was in operation. There was still enough room for a driveway around the new buildings to get to the diesel bowsers and rear parking areas. Billy then thought about his mobile trading vans, maybe some of them should be available again, although this area was out of their normal range and the fairgrounds were still running in season.

Mathew and Beth weighed in to the argument and decided to find out where the fairground was operating at the moment and go for a drive out there and talk to the operators who had obliged last time. Beth went through Billy's office until she found the relevant details. She believed that they would only need two vans this time because the kitchen would still be operating for take-away meals and drinks both hot and cold. As it turned out the fairground was not too far away so they took a day off and went for a drive. They first approached the baked dinner van and the operator was delighted to see them. He shouted them a very nice lunch and because it was to be 24 hour trading he was keen to participate. The owner took them over to the Chinese take-away for a chat with the owner operator of that van and persuaded him to come along to Grantham as well. Mathew told them that they would only need the two vans this time to work in with their kitchen. Mathew and Beth spent an hour or two at the fairground before returning home.

The timing of all these changes fitted into their lifestyles because Mathew had been seriously courting a lovely girl, Evelyn, who also worked at the café as a senior cook. They were about to get engaged to marry so this new venture could possibly fit in well so long as they continued along those lines, and Beth was deeply, madly in love with the son of local business man, who was yet to step up and pop the question but might just do that if he could see a way forward. He was the second son of three so there would be no possible family friction if he moved away, from; not only the family home, but even the town and district. Robert was getting a bit despondent with Beth disappearing regularly. They hardly spent any time together these days and as soon as they got possession of the accommodation this weekend Beth and Matt would be camping at the road house continuously. There was a worry in Robert's mind that a beautiful and well set up young lady like Beth could easily be tempted away to new pastures and leave him behind. When he realised that Beth would now have a suitable home and a great career he needed to move quickly. He had loved Beth ever since the day that she started at the high school and although he was two years her senior he was badly smitten with her. For nearly seven years Robert had doted on Beth and he decided that now was the time to move in and cement the deal before some other young fellow did.

The next weekend he had promised to take her out dancing which he did, then on the way home he popped the question and was eagerly accepted. They decided to talk to Matt and Evelyn about the possibility of a double engagement party at the restaurant and of course Matt agreed. When Beth came around later in the day they approached Mel and Billy who were delighted and congratulated them on their decision. Billy said, "That's great news so that you can start at Grantham as equal partners if that's what you want and we'd better begin organising a wedding ceremony soon. No sense hanging about since you'll have a nice refurbished home, with all mod cons, all set up ready to move into. You'd better get married and enjoy a honeymoon straight away because once the new place is finished I doubt you'll have much time for leisure."

The old family gang of helpers geared up for the assault on the new venue. Fred, Alison, Melissa, and all the in-law families. Gwen and John, Evelyn's parents joined in with Robert's parents, Nancy and Peter as they shouldered arms and attacked the existing living quarters to bring them up to date and make them liveable. It was amazing what a good clean out and a lick of paint can do to a room. With new curtains and floor coverings each room soon became home or at least part of it. The kitchens were rebuilt to modern standards as were bathrooms and toilets. There were two separate dwellings which had had shared ablutions but now, would be entirely independent except for a large laundry facility between them.

Chapter Thirteen

The business buildings were progressing flat out and would be finished by the engagement weekend which would be celebrated at the Restaurant in Haversby.

The new café/restaurant and service station was progressing apace. The fuel companies joined forces to provide first rate facilities at the front for smaller vehicles and around the rear for diesel vehicles. Billy had decided to go the whole hog and build a two story premises with a classy upmarket restaurant on the upper floor where there were magnificent views of the surrounding countryside.

The Roadhouse and Restaurant near Haversby was fast becoming famous for its celebrative dinners and evenings of fun and games and dancing. Not only was this the sixth of such family events but there had been quite a number celebrated by other local members for birthdays, engagements, weddings, and funerals and christenings and any other excuse that the locals could dream up for a night out on the town.

As they did in Sheffield, Billy organised a clearing sale to get rid of old furniture, fittings and trappings at Grantham. Once again he was amazed at what sort of goods could be sold at auction, some of it, at, or even above normal retail price, even after paying commissions they were greatly pleased with the outcome and immediately began sourcing new furniture and fittings for, not only the cafe, but also the residences. Mel, Beth, Nancy, and Alison went on a shopping safari mainly for the residences because Billy had already contacted the wholesale suppliers who looked after the Sheffield refit and they were eager to participate again and had already been to the site to measure up. Also he had contacted Roystons Amusements about a new jukebox and late model electronic poker machines. The existing café was already equipped with older versions of these machines which meant that the council approval was securely in place already. Roystons indicated that it was new territory for them but they were happy to usurp the predecessors and snaffle their site. This meant that Matt and Beth had access to the very latest machines and recordings in both areas.

The existing amusement supplier was not at all happy to lose this outlet, although he did allow that he had been quite lackadaisical in his approach to the venue and to his business in general. He had been in the business for many years and was now getting tired and nowhere near as active as he should be. As the machines aged they became less reliable which meant that he was running back and forth trying to keep them operating. He was active only in his regular collection of monies from the old machines but he was no longer prepared to keep recapitalizing the outfit to keep it up to date. He admitted that he didn't have any of the latest jukeboxes and his music collection was long out of date.

When queried about the poker machines, he owned up to the fact that he himself had no knowledge or expertise in the electronics of these new era machines so when, they gave trouble, he would have to call in electronic experts or engineers to maintain them at considerable cost. He stated that the amusement industry was now a young man's game. He shook hands with Billy and Mathew and began to remove his machines to make way for the new ones from Roystons The installers from Roystons were quite happy to assist the old bloke with the removal and transportation of his ancient machines and even suggested that they could be in a position to take over his territory and clients. Many of his machines were of vintage quality but small village pubs and clubs and cafes might be able to absorb the best of them. Roystons could and did in fact send their team of sales people to the new territory and they were soon in a position to update many of the older machines. A good many of the older machines actually found new homes nearby and after a good clean up, both internally as well as externally, and a full service and update of records and machinery, meant they still had a profitable life ahead of them.

The grand opening at Grantham was to be a repeat of the celebrations in the two previous venues. The advertising and public participation reviews in the "Headlight' Magazine were second to none so, hopefully, all their driver friends and other new comers would get excited and come along for a fun weekend and heaps of good grub. Billy even arranged to have a number of fairground rides and entertainments for the kiddies. Fairy floss, popcorn, toffee apple, and hot chips, always went well and might, and even did, entice more of the locals to become imbued with the advantages of the new premises, such as the store and modern jukebox and great dining experience.

The ground floor was exactly what the truckers and travelling motorists needed and the upper floor was ready for the better class of serious diners. Mathew and Beth were hoping to repeat the dining experience of Haversby and were prepared for formal parties, celebrations, weddings and more. On weekends when no other events were proposed Mathew organised suitable bands or orchestras to provide music for dinner dance routines which were winners in their own right, By opening night they had already received a number of suggested dates for formal dinner parties to test out the advertising hype.

Meanwhile there was a double engagement to celebrate at Haversby and many of the lorry drivers were on hand to wish the happy couples all the very best for their future together.

Once the two engagement parties were over the next question was the double wedding. Both young couples welcomed the idea so plans were put about to make it happen sooner rather than later. With both couples planning to settle into the new roadhouse together it seemed imperative that little or no time was wasted. Both of the bridal partners would be working together in the new café so they needed to be living close together. At the engagement party Mathew and Evelyn agreed on a future date for their wedding day. Before the night was over, Robert and Bess agreed to double up with them to save time and money. Both couples were adamant that the wedding celebrations would be held in the newly completed restaurant at Grantham.

Melissa and Billy as one would expect realised that this would be a great event to show case their new facilities in Grantham and set out to organise a great evening. Still with the weddings and Billy accepted the invitation to "Give Away' his lovely daughter knowing full well that Robert would succour and defend her til death doth them part He believed they would make a great team both business wise and personally. Similarly John stepped up to do the honours for his daughter Evelyn. The family ladies were going flat out preparing the brides and grooms whilst Billy, John and Peter tackled the job of making this a day to be remembered. Old Fred was not to be denied and joined in with all his skills to make the new restaurant something very special for the day and for the future. Of course Phil and his staff got involved with a flower show to equal any ever seen in this town. They set up all the trappings to showcase their combined businesses on this special day. The wedding ceremony at the family church in Haversby was set for 11 am on the Saturday morning with the wedding breakfast set for 4 pm to allow travelling time between the two towns and the general public were invited to attend a free dinner dance starting about 7 pm that evening, until very late. Once the dancing was well on the way the bridal couples went home to change before their departure They cut into the wedding cakes and shared them around the guests before departing, for a well earned rest and honeymoon. It was a good job that Billy and Melissa with assistance from their staff had made not one but two huge three tiered cakes because the hall was full and bursting at the seams. As Mathew said to his family just before leaving, "If this shindig hasn't set us on the road to success, nothing ever will. Thank you Mum and Dad for all this. The business the wedding and now an evening like this to launch our futures together. Thanks a million. We love you both and all our family."

Elizabeth and Robert joined Billy and Melissa for another session of cuddles, kisses and thank you messages then the two couples left the ball as they headed off out of town. They had to stop before travelling too far to remove all the good wishes trailing from their cars rear bumpers. Everyone else walked back inside to continue the fun.

Once the weddings were over and done with it was back to business. Many of their lorry driver friends accompanied by their fellow drivers quickly espoused the much awaited and rebuilt venue. As before most of the professional drivers pointed out that they relied on the various roadhouses to, not only fuel up their lorries and fill their bellies, but also to fill out their personal lives and fill the gaps between home comforts and business times. They said it was good to feel wanted, and welcome, and be part of the outfit, not just a source of revenue for the owners. Their main need however, was top quality menus, and food selections to whet their appetites, and not provide them with a good solid dose of indigestion and acid reflux as they drove along.

As Billy and Mel had researched the town they realised it needed a top of the class dining venue, with ample parking to fill their leisure times. At weekends Mathew organised local bands to provide live music well into the night and there was plenty of space to trip the light fantastic once the dining tables had been rearranged after the meals were finished. Farther more, because the restaurant was a short way out of town and the nearest residents were far enough away not to be disturbed by loud noises, their late night activities did not upset anyone. The main railway lines between London and Edinburg actually ran right through the town anyway, creating a hideous intermittent racket. The flying Scotsman was amongst these trains and it did not stop in Grantham as did the Leeds and York express trains.

Mathew and Evelyn set about inciting the locals to shop at their retail store and word soon circuited the town and nearby villages telling of the freshness and quality of the products on hand; plus out of season flowers and fruits, as well as very competitive prices so it was only a matter of time before it began to happen and soon they were searching for more staff for the tills and other domestic work needed to run the shop. Some of the handicapped people were more than willing to step up to clear all the domestic work around the store and the residences. Some of the handicapped personnel were given the tasks of flower arranging and presenting the vegetables for sale. Mat and Eve realised that a person did not even need two or even one leg to sit all day before the tills and fuel consoles so they were trained to do so. They only needed wheelchair access to their work stations and they were away. Most of the customers had no idea that the console operator had only one and sometimes no legs at all.

Phil had organised a delivery schedule to supply Mathew with fresh flowers, plants vegetables and fruit. The local supplier was not best pleased to be ousted from this lucrative trade but Matt was astute enough to turn it around. He installed a new cool-room at the rear of the café from where he was able to wholesale Phil's produce direct to the shops in the town and surrounding villages with twice weekly deliveries of fresh produce, the green grocer could easily compete with his rivals.

Life quickly settled into a pleasant routine and Evelyn took time out to visit the schools and colleges as Billy had done in Haversby, with a view to get students to work and train with them at the café and roadhouse and learn to become suitable employees.

As in most country towns reasonably qualified and experienced, cooks, chefs, kitchen hands, and especially key board console operators, to handle the new style tills, were as prevalent as rocking horse manure and hens teeth. Evelyn astounded the town's principal teachers but it only took a few weeks for them to realise what was being offered. As one headmaster stated, "We are here to teach our students certain social skills, however our primary duty is to prepare them to join the work force and earn a decent living once school is finished. Because your roadhouse operates 24hrs every day we can allow our students to spend training time with you and still manage full time schooling. Yes please Evelyn, bring it on and we'll cooperate with you all the way."

Once the system began students in other schools and colleges begged to transfer to this school so other head teachers had, although reluctantly, adopted the scheme and the obvious result was a big drop in youth unemployment in the area, a reduction in vandalism, graffiti, and other antisocial behaviour in the towns. This continual stream of students did not only benefit the roadhouse. Once trained up to Mathew's standards, the young people were able to take up employment anywhere in the district so they could select a job close to their homes, if they needed to. The till and checkout skills were needed in most shops and business premises anywhere in the country and Mathew heard that many businesses were demanding a copy of his certificate of competence before employing any new employees. This demonstrated to the possible employer that, at least, the applicant could be relied upon to work diligently, be polite and respectful to their customers, as well as operate a qwerty keyboard competently. Reading this report you might be silly enough to believe that Mathew's schooling was a total success but it was far from that. Some of the students, in spite of careful vetting by the school's teaching staff, just weren't prepared to knuckle down and learn anything, so they were dismissed as total failures. The roadhouse provided a number of different work opportunities so any-one who could not find a niche in or around it were destined to fail in life. They were in for huge shocks later in life when they found out that there were no jobs for their types of youngsters. They were destined for the dole queues or council workers, maybe for life. Mathew was disappointed each time this happened, not because he felt sorry for the student involved, but because some other student had been robbed of the chance to try.

The new roadhouse settled down without too many glitches and was soon showing a steady profit. After being married for over twelve months both couples decided to try for babies. This baby business seldom occurs to plan but Matt and Eve were first cab off the rank but it took them four months for it to happen. Robert and Beth were getting a bit despondent because they hadn't managed to conceive in the next three months, when suddenly they began to relax and soon fell pregnant. Mathew pointed out that the timing was great because they didn't want both of their ladies to present at the same time. The four months interval would give them time to adjust and share the load, both at the roadhouse and at home.

Eventually, Evelyn presented Matt with a full term, bouncing, baby, boy much to everyone's delight especially the grandparents. The baby was christened Paul Michael Riley. All the ladies involved in the family circles took turns to squat at the roadhouse and babysit. Just as they were getting this little one sorted out Beth went into labour and she also gave birth to a little boy who they named Charles Ronald Wilson.

Very belatedly, Billy settled down to normal work again and his first call was to wander down through the market gardens and greenhouses where he hoped to catch up with Phil who had been sadly neglected in recent times but the extra business was a great bonus to him and his crew.

Billy found Phil in the mushroom warehouse with the girls Gwen and Gladys discussing where to go next. The whole project was a winner on all fronts but it was necessary to keep abreast with current trends. They needed to look at different varieties and more housing. Billy jumped in as far as the growing sheds were concerned by pointing out that the farm where they had procured the greenhouses was now a housing estate meaning that all the farm buildings were empty or as it turned out just storage areas for assorted junk and unused rusty machinery. The farm homestead was very close to the existing farm and almost next door in fact. Unknown to Phil and the girls, old Joseph, the farmer in question, had approached Billy about disposal of some or all the machinery. Billy was certain that with a good overhaul the forklift still had plenty of service life as with much of the other machines and tools.

Billy said, "How about you guys take a bit of time off now and we can all go over there and have a brain tank to see if any of the buildings and plant are useful before he offers it elsewhere; or calls an auction sale. They climbed into Phillips vehicle for the short drive to Joseph's place. There was quite a lot of machinery of various descriptions most of which was virtually scrap as far as Phil and Billy were concerned but still had use for hay making and grain growing so they cleaned it all up and sold off any superfluous to their needs and prepared the rest for their own use.

There were two tractors, one quite small and another later model of around 40 hp, both of which would be great assets to their outfit once cleaned up and serviced. There was a plough or two, a scarifier and sets of harrows as well as a crop sprayer and seed drill. The unwanted machinery and tools Phil sold off and shared the spoils with Joseph.

The girls were in raptures of delight over the various barns and other buildings. Now at last they could extend their operations and spell some of the sheds making them easier to clean and keep repaired. They were keen to get started so Billy caught up with Joseph and Marion, his wife, to draw up suitable lease details to put the operation on a proper footing, although Joseph didn't believe it was necessary, between friends and neighbours. Billy pointed out to them that if and when anything happened to them he needed to be assured of a continuation of the arrangement for posterity because the firm needed to spend a good deal of money on upgrades and repairs. As it turned out the old couple changed their will and turned everything; including the big house over to Billy and Melissa. Joseph and Marion now only own and work the block of land encompassing their generous farm house, as well as all the extensive surrounding buildings. There were two workers cottages alongside the extensive barns which would need refurbishing before becoming a valuable part of Billy's estate, a large orchard, containing many fruit trees, all of which needed to be heavily pruned and fertilised. and two small fields of about ten acres each.

Exiting as all this was Phil, Fred Vanessa and Alison declared that they were all too old for anymore ventures and Billy would need to utilise the younger members of his family and friends, along with contractors and field workers. That all suited Billy, and he rounded up a team of workers to begin the changes and renovations. The two fields were ploughed up manured and prepared for spring crops. The orchard was to be thoroughly pruned and manured ready for spring sunshine to invigorate the trees. To this end Billy visited the senior schools and colleges to suggest a training workshop for some of their senior students, and this was gladly accepted. However, time was limited and the weather waited for no-one. In spite of his declaration Phil appeared on a regular basis mainly to advise the students on the various techniques regarding pruning, budding, and grafting, as well as espalier training; and to keep an eye on the field preparations, although Jeffry was very experienced in this task he welcomed any input from Phil. Jeff loved ripping up stagnant ground and re-enervating it into a productive cropping medium and these two fields hadn't been worked for a good many years, if ever. The rich soil full of years of animal manure would make excellent potato and root crops; followed by a crop of winter greens. The café could always use large quantities of potatoes and frequently needed to buy in large quantities in the off season. However with a huge crop of their own which was easily stored in one of the barns they would even be able to sell some around the town.

Adrian and Allan declared that they still had plenty of go in their bodies and were soon hard at work preparing the cottages for staff accommodation and the buildings to increase the mushroom business. Old Fred couldn't stay away for long and he often appeared with Phil to survey the work and help with suggestions concerning the refurbishing of the cottages and redecorating the rooms. Fortunately most of the young members of the teams and even some of the handicapped personnel were extra keen to get the project on schedule because it meant more permanent jobs for the other employees and students.

The good times had rolled on too long and inevitably there was bound to be some serious glitches in the scheme. The first glitch came in the way of a desperate phone call from Mathew to his dad, Billy. One of his staff was having frequent bouts of nausea and vomiting so Beth drove her to see their Doctor just to make sure of her own diagnosis and was proved correct. The girl was definitely pregnant but fortunately not to any of the other members of the staff. Mathew asked his dad;"What can I do to sort out the mess? Could I in fact, terminate her employment and replace her with a reserve because it is totally unsuitable to have a member of staff vomiting in the kitchen." Billy and Melissa had a long talk and decided that the girl would have to stay on at the café as long as she could still carry out her duties. Melissa suggested that Beth should drive the girl to her parent's home and discuss the situation with them. She was terrified of her dad's reaction but Mel said they would have to know sooner or later and see what could be sorted out; and the sooner the better for all concerned. Beth took the girl home and weathered the explosions until they all quietened down. The parents thanked Beth for her care and attention and promised to take over the responsibility for their wayward daughter. As far as Matt and Beth were now concerned all they needed to do was rearrange the staff rosters and move one of their trainees up to fill the gap. Thank goodness the student training scheme was working extremely well and they always had replacement staff in times of sickness and holidays.

The next concern for Billy and Melissa and to a lesser extent Phil was the intimacy between the two mushroom girls. They had all been aware of a certain amount of intimacy between the girls who shared accommodation as well as their workplace. Billy and Melissa had discussed the possibility of a closer relationship between the two women but they reckoned that so long as they were very discreet it was none of their business, and who cared what they did in private. Their input was so valuable to the firm. Those two girls consistently produced a huge quantity of top-of-the-range products which were instantly saleable. Above that their self trained skills were almost impossible to replicate although other staff members were working alongside them to gain the knowledge and experience necessary to take over from time to time, and help out at busy times. There had been a certain amount of malicious gossip about the pair so that Mel and Billy decided to spend a little time with the women and explain the problem to them. They did not deny their relationship and promised to be much more discreet in the future.

About one year after the birth of Matt and Beth's babies both ladies became pregnant again and Malcolm and Rosalind already had two boisterous boys and a sweet little girl, which they decided was quite enough for them to cope with and sometimes too much. They were doing such a fantastic job of running the Sheffield roadhouse that Mel and Billy only needed to make short and very occasional visits up there, to help and advise. That, more than anything else gave them lots more time to assist their kids with the Roadhouse at Grantham although Matt and Evelyn were doing a really great professional job over there, with very little assistance from home With all three roadhouses now running like clockwork Billy was able to spend much of his time involved with the refurbishment project at Joseph's, Avon Valley Farm.

The whole set up at Avon Valley was extraordinary with so many barns and buildings to play with and the fields were showing great promise. Phillip couldn't help himself although he was past doing the manual work he was heavily engaged in the planning and planting routines. The cut flower business was going ballistic these days so they planted acres of chrysanthemums corn flowers dahlias and even roses and many other varieties including a number of non-flowering plants like ferns, to provide foliage, only. Phil was slowly managing to get suitable staff, mostly women, who were interested and keen to take over from him in the green house management, The whole project and especially the potted flowering plants and to a lesser extent tomatoes needed serious dedication to get the timing correct and end up with a viable profitable output. Likewise the extended mushroom business was going like clockwork with only minimal help from Billy and Mel but it needed a very dedicated team to assure a continuous output. As one of the ladies commented, "It's worse than looking after a house full of new born babies. One tiny mistake and you end up with a greenhouse full of composting material. They decided to have only the one slicing and packaging depot and that was moved over to the Avon Valley farm into one of the massive stone barns, which have much improved access and far more space so the machines weren't jammed in on top of each other, and with good walking space all around them.

One of the biggest headaches surrounding agriculture and horticulture was the advent of the European Common Market. That organisation consumed a great deal of time and much heartache. Billy and Phil were able to negate a large part of the problems because they mainly produced goods exclusively for their own use and needed no part of the marketing arrangements. However there were some problems at all their outlets because they supplied many of the local shops directly from their cool rooms on site. The main thing that the common market did for England was to create many new jobs for clerical workers. The common market demanded a huge amount of paperwork to control the output and input of the stock at each and every facet of the food movement program until it was finally sold at retail. Much of the products that Billy and Phil dealt with were not included in the common market system because much of their production, like mushrooms and out of sequence horticulture; such as out of season flowers plants and fruits, were marketed when no other product was available so they got away with 'murder'. Unfortunately the common market insisted that all their production had to be documented and copies sent to head office in Brussels just to keep the clerks and bean counters over there busy even out of season. Melissa could manage to cope with the enormous amount of paperwork surrounding the handicapped people whom they employed on top of all the normal in-house paperwork, wages accounts etc. but the common market necessitated the need for one dedicated staff member and a vehicle to travel around their three businesses on a regular basis to document all the movement of stock from place to place. Fortunately, they were already employing a lady of almost thirty years of age who had much clerical experience prior to moving to Haversby recently. She was wasted in the greenhouses; and did not enjoy the experience either, but she knuckled down to the work and was quite competent and became highly involved in a very short period of time. Mavis was delighted to take on the clerical work and loved to drive so Billy escorted her around until she was competent with the nature of the demands of the EEC and protocol needed to keep them happy. She set up check sheets at each venue, collated all the information, made out comprehensive reports and submitted copies of them to the relevant offices and bombarded them with so much [too much] information that they kept out of her way.

In the early days of parenthood Melissa and Billy believed that in the ideal world they could provide a living and life style for all their offspring, but as one would imagine that was never going to happen, Their kids each had minds of their own with different career paths, hopefully to fame and fortune. Whilst Mathew and Elizabeth were equally keen on cooking and restaurant experiences, Marion had much different expectations in life. She showed interest in nursing and healing the sick people and animals in her busy little life. She and her school friends were often seen in one of the semi-vacant rooms in the old farm house where they set up "hospitals" for their dolls and sometimes reluctant pets. There was plenty of oft unused furniture in the attics which they dragged around the house to establish nursing wards and even operating theatres. Old curtains were hung around the rooms for privacy and they found much of the paraphernalia needed in a busy hospital stored in the attics.

By the time she and one or two of her friends settled down to obtain their GCE's, which were essential to qualify to enter the sacred halls of nursing, they were determined that they would enter that hallowed profession and her friends actually did that; however Marion realised that she was destined for greater heights and stayed at Grammar school until she earned her "A" levels with flying colours and applied for university entrance to study to become a family doctor. She was accepted into Birmingham University medical faculty where she worked like a demon. She was determined to be the best of the group and even beat all the male members of their grade. There were only two young ladies in the group but that only made her even more determined to be the best. She eventually completed her studies and qualified with "Honours". Birmingham suited Marion best because there was a direct passenger service between home and college enabling her to escape regularly to keep in touch with her much loved family. By the time that Marion entered college she, like her dear Mum was a very beautiful young lady who loved to dance, especially ballroom but apart from using the young men in her life as dancing partners she shouldered off each and every aspirant for her favours. She was going to be the top qualifier for a position in her chosen career and no young man would get a look in until that happened.

Once qualified she applied for and obtained a top position as intern in the big hospital in Birmingham. At that time women doctors were still not readily accepted in the medical world but Marion's qualifications carried her through. Marion still continued to study with a view to becoming a senior doctor and she specialised in women's medicine and especially midwifery and all its associated complications.

Whilst his big sister was blitzing the medical world Michael had followed suit up to a certain point. He had indulged in all the medical games with his sister and friends but he escaped to a nearby farm owned by a class mate's family on a regular basis where he was able to follow his more fitting interests. The farm was a mixed animal farm with a herds of sheep and pigs, intermingled with a large assortment of poultry. The farm even included a few milking cows and a couple of horses. Michael was determined to equal his sister but he would become a veterinary surgeon and care for animals. Small pet animal work was becoming very prevalent by then and much more lucrative than farm work although he would be involved with both sides of this great profession. The small animal work, although often quite tedious and fiddly, was much less stressful on his body than the equivalent work on large farm animals, like cows and horses, with their owners being much more attached to their animals they were more inclined to fork out large quantities of money to save them and keep them alive. Small dogs and cats for example and even pet birds were treated like children and sometimes better than children. Often a farmer has to consider the sale value of; say a pregnant ewe or even a dairy cow before deciding to spend hundreds of pounds on a caesarean section or a broken leg. It was far more pleasant operating on a dog in the surgery or even in the owners house than crawling about in mud, ice or even snow in a remote stone barn on a freezing winter night with the East wind tearing at your clothing and often bare arms and chest.

Of course all that was still to come and Michael had first to gain entry to the university and Vet school and pass with top honours to even be able to operate on animals. Even with very good qualifications, getting a place with a practicing Veterinary Surgeon was not always possible. At least his family had plenty of backing and would be able to set up and equip a surgery in one of the nearby towns where there would be plenty of small animal work to make a good living.

At the time that Michael qualified he was only able to work for a pittance of a wage in a large country practice where he was being unfairly treated; being forced out in all weathers to handle all the rough jobs that the practice owner didn't want to handle himself. Michael tolerated this treatment for a while because he was gaining lots of valuable experience until

Melissa, his mum rang him one day asking for him to visit that weekend. Michael drove his van home on the Friday after work, much to the ire of his boss who was left with all the nasty jobs for the weekend.

Melissa and Billy were so glad to see him home even for a short spell because besides missing him so badly they had a proposition for him. An elderly vet with a practice outside Moreton-in-the marsh had had a vigorous business but was too elderly and infirm to cope with much of it even before he received a kick from a cart horse which mangled up his knee. The vet in question lived in a large country house with the surgery included. He was employing a very competent receptionist cum nurse and needed someone urgently to carry on the work and preferably to buy the outfit, either just the business, or preferably, the whole outfit, house, surgery, and land; whilst it was still a vibrant operation. Billy had already spoken to his bank manager and organised for the transfer of capital provided a suitable deal could be reached.

Billy asked Michael how things stood at his present location. Michael grinned from ear to ear as he reported that his boss would only take him on as a casual assistant so he had no hold over him what-so-ever. He said he would drive over there early the next morning collect his tools and paraphernalia as well as his clothes and leave immediately. He pointed out that he was owed a small amount in wages but he would sacrifice that if necessary. Billy decided to run Michael back to his place of work, assist him to pack, and demand the wages owing. When they arrived the vet's wife was holding the fort because her husband had been called out to a big operation and would not be back for some time. Michael demanded the rest of his wages collected his belongings and walked out amidst much protestation and verbal abuse but he was entirely satisfied with the outcome.

They called in at home on the way through for lunch then continued on to Moreton-in-the marsh. They were greeted with much enthusiasm and given the grand tour. Michael was a bit disappointed with the presentation of buildings, surgery and surrounds but as Billy said, "We have sorted much worse than this son and with friends like Allan and his dad we can and will get it sorted. You just keep the business side of things operating and we'll do the rest. You can board here with Marissa and Ken until we get some of the rooms up to scratch." Because Michael had all his belongings and tools on board he was able to jump in and assist with the practice immediately whilst Billy discussed the sale details with Marissa. They each telephoned their solicitors and agreed to meet at the surgery the next day to sort out the details whilst Michael moved into one of the spare bedrooms and took over the snug for his temporary office. Marissa was delighted to have Michael on board immediately to save the business and take away the stress from both herself and Ken.

It turned out that Marissa and Ken had been thinking about retiring for some time and they had decided on where they would move to and had actually put in an offer for a neat little cottage nearby. Once Ken was fully mobile again he would be able to act as a relief Vet for surgery work and give Michael the benefit of his many years of practice. The receptionist was more than ready to welcome Michael into the fold because she was already sick of putting off their desperate clients and juggling the schedules around Ken's disability. Billy had already spoken to Allan and his dad and they were keen to get involved. Adrian was not as fit as he was but Allan was extra keen and he had built up a decent team of tradesmen to work with him including a painter and plumber.

There was a decent sized room next to the surgery which Allan and crew attacked first to create an operating theatre, complete with sterilisers and an anaesthetic machine. The practice only handled emergencies at the weekends so the builders and painters soon had the waiting rooms and day surgery up to date. Billy rounded up a team of his garden workers `to attack the grounds and gardens and rake the gravel driveways and parking areas. The painters concentrated on the inside of the house and surgery then moved outside to get stuck into the exterior which was quite a mess. There was enough work for them inside so they were able to work outside when the weather permitted then hide inside on the bad days. Ken was amazed at how quickly the place was taking shape and he managed as best he could with his wheel chair restrictions to assist Michael both inside the surgery and on his trips around the district where most of the clients lived and operated.

Billy had been busy sorting out the Veterinary business that he nearly missed a looming catastrophe. His favourite butcher, Michael, had decided to retire. He was not fit enough to handle carrying the bodies of meat around anymore so he negotiated a sale with a young, out-of-town recently qualified butcher. This should not have caused too many problems for Billy because Michael's assistant, Ian continued to work with the new owner, however that's where the problems began. The new proprietor thought himself the expert in everything. I must hereby define the term expert for those in doubt; we all know 'X' is an unknown entity and a spurt is merely a drip under pressure. He wanted to change everything including Billy's recipes for sausages and hamburger mince. He disallowed Ian to cut the small thin steaks and chops and threw away most of the bones. They were into the third week when Billy's staff alerted him to the practice so he went around to meet the new owner and try to sort out the mess but the butcher pointed out to Billy that he was the boss and his staff did as he told them or they could bugger off. This left Billy in a quandary. He did not want to change his winning formula so he went around to Michael's home for a chat. Michael told him "Change butchers Billy. It's that simple. He'll soon come around, you see if he doesn't."

Billy replied, "It won't be temporary if I do. I never want to see that pig again"

Michael's reply was "Do it Billy it won't affect me, I've been paid out in full. My only concern is for Ian but he's a smart cookie and will sort himself out in time."

Billy said , "I've had a couple of visits from a young butcher who's struggling to set up in Norton and was finding it hard going because you had all the best business in the area. Do you know anything about him by any chance."

"I know he only buys the best meat from the same place as I did. I met him there a time or two and I'd be game to give him a go, although

I pity the poor sod if he has to deal with you to make a living."

"Now then Michael don't start that again, that's my tactic as you well know, but I'll drive out to see his shop and set up, thanks for your help.

Billy went straight out to Norton and found the butcher's shop. The owner was Paul Godfrey and he did seem pleasant. Billy had a good look around before he introduced himself and explained his predicament. Paul was eager to work with Billy but was a bit reticent until he knew how big the business was. He was stunned to find out that Billy ran three roadhouses and three retail shops as well. Billy pointed out that it wouldn't be new business for the abattoir because that's where his meat was sourced anyway and it only needed to be re-routed from one shop to another. He then pointed out that his refrigerated lorries went passed the abattoir and the shop at Norton so they would deliver the raw carcasses and collect and deliver the orders for all three outfits. Billy also told Paul about Ian and his small goods and he reckoned that he would already be keen to move on. Billy soon convinced Paul that he could manage the extra business and he would buffer him against the sudden volume changes to prevent any financial mishaps. Finally Paul asked, "I don't understand Billy, what's in this for you?"

"Very simple; it takes me back to where I started, provided you meet my requirements. Firstly I want to see that pig of a butcher go arse up, and I want to return the many favours Michael and Ian heaped on me over the years, and more than anything, I need a butcher who can deliver quality meat into my establishment on a regular basis. At a fair and reasonable price. My meat supply is my life line, my guarantee of quality, My lorry drivers depend on me to feed them top quality produce and I will, even if I have to set up my own butchers shop to do it. So do we have a deal?"

"You bet your life on it and I'll do my very best to honour that, do you need anything today whilst you're here?" Between them they built up an order to replace the Haversby stock and Billy left an order for the rest of the week. Until Paul could upgrade his staff he was going to be run off his feet but then Billy decided to rearrange his schedule so he could be in Norton the next morning to re-hone his butchering skills. Hopefully the abattoir would be able to provide the extra bodies for this time at least.

His small goods would be a problem for a day or two but Billy was sure he could change that scenario quite quickly. He returned back to the café and loaded up all the meat left over from the mornings delivery and replaced it with the product from Paul's place. Then he drove around to the butcher's rear entrance and returned all the stock along with the invoices and cancelled all future orders. The butcher was still jumping up and down and shouting his head off when Billy stepped outside. As he passed Ian he quietly asked him to call at the roadhouse on his way home. The next thing, he put all his butchering tools in his car alongside the sausage recipe and a box of assorted herbs and spices. At about 6pm Ian drove in and found Billy; asking him what was happening. He told Billy that his boss had gone mad when Billy walked out and he was still ranting and raving when Ian walked out at the end of his shift.

Billy asked if he could spare an hour or two and offered him the use of the phone to check in at home. They drove off to Norton with Billy filling in the gaps of the day's events. Paul was still hard at work trying to make up for time lost. The abattoir had done a quick delivery bringing all the bodies he had asked for so he pitched in to try and get ahead again. Billy passed a couple of his knives and a steel to Ian who began trimming the carcasses and boning some parts to get enough meat for the sausages. Billy, much to Pauls amazement set to with a will breaking up bodies to obtain the cuts that he needed and plenty of bones. Billy and Ian had driven up in one of the refrigerated vans which they loaded for the return journey home. Ian had the mincer and sausage maker running flat out and the others supplied him with trimmed meat. He soon had little sausages hanging everywhere whilst Billy cut up lamb chops and mutton chunks and Paul sliced and shaped small steaks and selected a few nice roasts to cook and slice for cold meat and salad dishes. There was a decent amount of bones, some of which Paul had cast aside during the day and would have dumped had not Billy turned up. Finally Billy stopped and demanded mugs of tea so they could discuss Ian's situation., He accepted a position with Paul who was still shaking his head in wonder at this nights work. They had changed a potential disaster into a great triumph in just a few hours. Billy and Paul put their heads together to work out a future basic order for all three roadhouses which needed to be shipped separately. Billy was able to supply a rough timetable for their vans to collect the orders and a second one to cover the delivery of bulk meat into the butcher's premises. The abattoir near Alcastor was only a slight deviation for the lorries on their return journey from the Sheffield café thus saving much time and delivery costs. Paul had finally added up the cost of the current consignment and Billy added a similar amount for the next one and wrote out a cheque to square the deal. As they were leaving Paul asked Ian about accommodation and travel expenses and suggested that there was plenty of room at his place and maybe Ian could board with them during the week and run home at the weekends.

* * *

For some time now Melissa and Billy had been discussing career opportunities for their youngest child Bobbie. It was obvious from his early days that Bobbie was a wizard with figures so the suggestions centred around those skills, including teacher, banker, accountant etc. Bobbie would be happy so long as there were ample amounts of figures to shuffle around but he finally sorted the problem himself. There were plenty of opportunities in the family businesses for someone with his accounting skills but he was looking for a career that would entertain his active mind, as well as reward him for his labours.

One day at his college he joined a young lady at lunch in the canteen. He apologised and asked if the other chair was taken and could he join her. She smiled at him and rearranged her belongings to give him room. She was one year older than him and very pleasant to look at. Bobby had been eyeing her off all that term but had no idea how to get to know her. They quickly shared names, hers was Belinda, and entered into general conversation. Belinda was madly studying mainly mathematics and English language as she was determined to join her parents in their insurance underwriting business which created heaps of travel, both in the UK but also abroad, mainly Europe at that time.

Robert and Belinda were enjoying each other's company and found that their individual lodgings were in the same building allowing them to spend lots of time together, both studying and socialising [snogging]. Bobby invited Belinda to spend some of their time off at the farm house and Belinda reciprocated with firstly weekends then part of the longer breaks to her home in Wolverhampton. Her father encouraged the pair to spend time in his office in the city and began tutoring both of them in the finer aspects of the underwriting business. Robert, although a year younger than Belinda, had a very outgoing nature which helped him to negotiate with the clients. A further benefit in Robert's favour was his language skills. At high school, much to his parents amazement he had taken extra studies in languages and had if fact obtained his 'O' level certificate in French, German and Italian. His Spanish was almost there but needed a little more work to which end he was planning to spend the next vacation in Spain, which would, hopefully, get him over the line for the future. After discussing the language problem with Belinda and Robert, George invited them both to spend the summer vacation with him in Spain where he kept a comfortable apartment on the coast.

Robert couldn't wait, he was desperate to spend time in Spain to brush up on the lingo and maybe meet other nationalities to improve his other language skills. As a result of all this George offered Robert a junior post in his insurance underwriting business where he fitted in well as did Belinda in spite of her language limitations. Robert specialised in the foreign offices where his language skills assisted the business. He became domiciled in France with his headquarters in the outskirts of Paris which was most convenient for access to the airport. He was covering much of southern France Spain and Italy with occasional sorties into Germany. Robert loved the work and intermingling with other people. Belinda spent much of her time at home base and eventually they met again in England. Both were unattached still, and Robert was now in his late twenties. Robert was recalled to head office for a serious conference in early May and he was to be picked up from Manchester airport to complete the journey.

Imagine his amazement and delight to find Belinda waiting for him at the airport. They were both thrilled and it took a good many serious kisses and much cuddling before they considered driving home

Robert had organised his office to get time off in England to catch up with family and friends and of course Belinda. It only took a day or two for Belinda and Robert to realise that they should be together for life. After a dual family conference a quick marriage service was organised and where-as the ceremony was brief the celebrations were not. Firstly a reception was held at the home of the bride with no expenses spared, then it was over to Haversby to another right royal shindig at the roadhouse mainly for the benefit of the Riley clan. That show was going exceptionally well until Billy rolled out the many tiered cake sculptured by his own hands. in the style of

Granny Elizabeth. Robert broke down in tears much to everyone's amazement. It was Melissa who first realised the problem as she rushed to his aide cuddled him into her arms and loved him dearly. Over his shoulder she mouthed to Billy, two words, "Granny Elizabeth".

Billy and the other Riley family members soon grasped the situation and carefully explained to Belinda's family and friends. It took a good many tears to console Robert before he and his bride were able to cut the cake. A good many of the assembled family also shed many tears in remembrance of Granny Elizabeth and her superb cakes. Once all the formalities were over, the bride and groom changed at the farm house before saying their final farewells back at the roadhouse and quickly bundled themselves into Billy's latest Jaguar for the trip to the airport and a flight to Paris for their honeymoon.

THE END.

BRIAN O'DONNELL
Author & Publisher
SHAKE RATTLE AND ROLL
ESCAPE From HELL
BRIAN O'DONNELL
YOU'VE GOT TO BE KIDDING
for inquiries:
bsodonsm@tpg.com.au
(08) 9531 4167

Escape from Hell

Escape from hell is the story of a teenage boy who has been cruelly and systematically belted by his father for little or no reason. He decides to leave home on his ancient bicycle towing a homemade trailer containing all his worldly belongings. He leaves home in the middle of the night and rides a few miles before the pain from his still bleeding belt wounds force him to rest. He has no safe haven to go to and distance is going to be his only ally. He's resting in the rear parking area of a 24 hour roadhouse in pouring rain when a sudden impulse shows him a method of escape. He takes the plunge and arrives at another 24 hour roadhouse over 200 miles away where he begins to make a new home for himself using the cooking skills taught by his mother and farming skills learned from his brutal father. He was used to working long hard hours in the harvest fields beside his father and he was astute enough to capitalize on the skills learned along the way. He made himself useful as a kitchen hand in the cafe.

Shake, Rattle and Roll

A 15 year old school boy is invited to become part of an exciting adventure extending over three summers in Yorkshire and Lancashire with touches of Durham and Northumberland thrown in along the way. Driving a steam driven, historical, agricultural tractor on iron wheels over vast distances each weekend to attend charity and historic rallies and _field days. Travelling over the Pennine Mountains and north Yorkshire moors to attend some of the greatest rallies and gala weekends ever experienced. He steered the tractor on some of the busiest roads in the north of England including many miles along the great north road now called the a1 highway, he guided his "charge" through many of the great industrial towns and cities of the north such as Leeds, Manchester, Newcastle, Durham and Chester-le-street.

Brian named his book "Shake Rattle and Roll" due to the discomfort of driving an iron monster on iron wheels with cross strakes.

You've Got To Be Kidding

My book contains [56] very readable, short, fun, stories about the many humorous situations that life has placed me in over the years. I have tried to introduce some of the quirky characters that I have met in my daily life. there were many very humorous incidents and others more startling and ghostly in character. However, life has a habit of delivering shattering blows to people and I was no exception to that rule, as will become obvious to my readers. In spite of all this, I believe that I have been much more fortunate than many others around me. I sincerely hope that you enjoy reading my stories as much as I enjoyed writing them.